When Love Calls

D1607695

by

Sharon C. Cooper

Disclaimer
This story is a work of fiction. Names, characters, and
incidents are either products of the author's imagination or
are used fictitiously. Any resemblance to actual events,
locales, organizations or persons, living or dead, is entirely
coincidental.

Dear Reader,

In *Love Under Contract*, book 1 of the Jenkins & Sons Construction series, I introduced Sumeera's parents: Russell McCray and Mona Gregory. I had no idea they would make such an impression on you! Since then, I have received a number of emails, asking about Mona's story and what happened after she walked away from Russell. In addition to those emails, several of you have requested that I write stories about more *seasoned* characters.

Well, I listened! Mona is a fifty-seven-year-old woman who has always wanted to get married and have a family. Instead, the man she ended up with showered her with every material thing a woman could want, but wasn't interested in marriage or having a large family. At first, that wasn't enough to make Mona leave him, but over the last few years, Russell has changed. And while he's not the same man she fell in love with, Mona realizes she's not the person she used to be either.

As for a new love interest for Mona...

If you're keeping up with the Jenkins & Sons Construction series, you'll recall that Mona was mentioned again in *Proposal for Love*. In that story, she caught the eye of Dexter Jenkins, a first cousin of Steven Jenkins. I loved Dexter from the moment I met him (smile). He's a cool *old dude* who has had some setbacks in life, but he's determined to move on and find a woman who is interested in starting a new chapter in her own life...with him. I figured, why not Mona.

I hope you enjoy Dexter and Mona's story!

Happy reading!

Sharon

Chapter One

"Russell was a selfish lover." Mona Gregory spoke the words to her sister and immediately wanted to pull them back. The comment was true. She just hadn't planned to voice them.

"And yet you stayed with the jerk for over thirty-five years," Johnette cracked, shaking her head.

No one understood that decision. On most days, not even Mona could come up with enough reasons on why she stayed. Her ex had been incapable of giving her what she wanted most—marriage and more children.

Weighed down with Nordstrom, Chicos, and Coach shopping bags, Mona and Johnette trudged through the parking lot at Kenwood Towne Centre. They'd been out for hours and Mona couldn't remember when she and her sister had spent so much time together. Johnette had flown into Cincinnati the day before from Puerto Vallarta, with plans to visit for two weeks. *Two weeks.* They had fourteen days to rebuild a relationship that had deteriorated over the last twenty-plus years.

"Watch that car." Johnette pulled on the back of Mona's jean jacket sleeve to keep her from stepping in front of a vehicle that rolled through a stop sign. "Idiot." Her sister glared at the driver, as if that would cause him remorse for almost running over someone.

"I think you parked over there." Mona tried pointing to their left but the bags banged together, hindering her from lifting her arm. Instead she nodded to the row where Johnette had parked the white rental car.

"I'll never understand you. If Russell couldn't even satisfy you sexually, what was the point?" Johnette picked up the conversation where they'd left off as they loaded the bags and climbed into the vehicle. "I'll admit the man is *fine*. And it doesn't hurt he has more money than Warren Buffett."

"He's not that rich," Mona mumbled, and fastened her seatbelt.

"Oh please. Condos on Central Park East aren't cheap. And apparently that, along with everything else he showered you with, was enough to keep you locked away from your family. And now I find out he wasn't even good in bed." She gave a disgusted chuckle and *tsked*. "He couldn't even get you off. Yet, you stayed."

Johnette steered the car toward the interstate that would take them to Mona's condo in Over-the-Rhine.

"Just drop it."

"I will not drop it. I live to talk about that loser. The guy is a pompous fool. Yet, you chose him over us, spending all those years separated from your family."

"Really? You act like I fell off the face of the earth or something. You could've called or visited New York whenever you wanted."

"And you could've done the same thing. Instead, you sacrificed everything, Mona, and for what? It's bad enough you cut me off, but Sumeera?" She pounded her hand on the steering wheel. "There's no way in hell I would've walked away or dumped my child on someone else in order to follow behind some guy."

Her sister was right. There was nothing Mona could say. She put Russell McCray first for most of her adult life and had more regrets than she could count. Her biggest—not maintaining a relationship with her daughter.

"He needed me. He was expanding the property development business, and there was a lot of traveling. Russell wanted me with him. At the time, I thought I was doing the right thing sending Sumeera to stay with you awhile, especially when we had to go overseas." Unfortunately, what was supposed to be a few weeks of Sumeera living with Johnette turned out to be six years.

Mona sighed at the memory. It was a miracle Sumeera had forgiven her and they were rebuilding their mother-daughter bond.

"That's all behind me now." Mona stared out the window, trying not to dwell on a past she couldn't change. Since reuniting with her daughter, she now had a new son-in-law, Nick, and a granddaughter, Chanelle.

She smiled to herself. Chanelle was the cutest baby Mona had ever seen and she had such a sweet disposition. Sumeera had been like that as a baby, only crying when she was hungry or wet. All other times, she was watchful and content.

"Now that you're free, what are you going to do with yourself? Cincinnati is a long way from New York."

Her new city was taking some getting used to, but leaving Russell and reconnecting with her family had been a good decision. And now that he had finally stopped calling, she could really move on.

"I'm planning to get a part-time job."

Johnette glanced at Mona, splitting her attention between her and the road. "I thought you said your investments were enough to live on. Why would you need to work?"

"I've been thinking about what I want to do with the rest of my life." At fifty-seven, she was finally ready to live her life and fulfill some of her dreams now that she had helped others. "Since I've always loved fashion, I want to eventually open up a boutique. But I figured it wouldn't hurt to work in retail awhile first."

Johnette's mouth dropped opened. "*Really?*"

"Yes, really. You don't have to sound so surprised. I know how to work and I know the basics about running a business. I played a major role in Russell's success."

Johnette shook her head. "Yeah, and I'm still shocked by that. All these years I assumed you were a kept woman, bowing down to your master."

"Would you knock it off with that crap? I'll admit that I stayed with Russell and put up with his nonsense for too long, but you and Sumeera act as if I didn't have a brain."

"What were we supposed to think, Mona? You followed behind him like some puppy dog. The few times either of us heard from you, it's not like you told us any different."

Mona stared down at her manicured hands folded in her lap. The royal blue tanzanite halo ring surrounded by diamonds stood out against her dark skin. The jewelry had been a gift from Russell on her last birthday. Since he made it very clear it was a gift and not an engagement ring, she wore it on her right hand.

She only had herself to blame for what Sumeera and Johnette thought of her. She knew part of her reason for staying with Russell was that he treated her well and showered her with the finer things in life. The first ten years, she saw it as his way of expressing his love for her, but each year reality set in. Sure, he loved her in his own way, but he never planned to love her the way she wanted to be loved. After a while, the years passed by in a blur. The older she got, the faster the days went, and before she knew it, she'd been with him for over thirty years.

"I'm going to start dating," she blurted.

"*What?*"

"Nothing serious, though. I've given up the whole matrimony idea. I don't need marriage. Besides, I'm tired of taking care of a man. I just want to meet some nice men. Preferably ones who are my age or younger. Someone I can go out with sometimes and maybe have, um, maybe have a sex partner." She looked everywhere but at her sister and ran her sweaty palms down her jean-covered thighs. She couldn't believe she was saying that out loud, even if it was true.

Johnette threw her head back and laughed as she exited the interstate. "So what you're telling me is that all you want from a guy is a friends-with-benefits setup? Someone to lube you up on occasion, like a mechanic or maintenance man?"

Mona frowned at her sister before laughing. "Well, when you put it like that, it sounds so…dirty."

Mona shivered, unable to keep the smile off her face. She would love to meet a man who was a little rough around the edges and had swagger. Someone who lived on the wild side—a little—and a man who could introduce her to new adventures. She had already experienced how the wealthy lived, traveling the continent, eating at the finest restaurants, and shopping at some of the most exclusive stores around the world. Now she wanted to live a simple, but enjoyable life and have some fun in the process.

"I know it sounds crazy, and I can't explain what's changed. All I know is that I want the freedom to do whatever I want without having to worry about a man's needs. You have enjoyed your life, coming and going as you please." At least that's how it was before Johnette met Carlos and moved to Puerto Vallarta a year ago to be with him. "I don't want to have to worry about if dinner is ready on time or host a dinner party for my man's business associates. I don't want to be tied down anymore."

"Who are you, and what have you done with my shy, prissy little sister?"

Mona laughed. Sure, she might be a little shy, and she couldn't deny that she was girly and maybe a little prim, but it was time she tapped into her other side. Her fun and exciting side. A side she wasn't sure existed, but she planned to find out.

*

Dexter Jenkins unlocked the door to his new home, overcome with a peace he hadn't felt in ages. For the past few years, he had lived in his daughter Katara's guest bedroom.

Though he felt at home with her and her husband and he enjoyed being around his grandchildren, he knew it had been time to get his own place.

"You definitely got the hook-up here, Dex. This is a nice size and it's cool you don't have to purchase all new furniture," Sean, Dexter's best friend since high school, said as he roamed around the partially furnished two-bedroom condominium, inspecting every inch of the place. "I need to see if I can get a gig like this."

Dex chuckled, grateful for his mechanical skills that he had picked up during his army days and during the years he worked for Jenkins & Sons Construction. Being good with his hands had landed him the caretaker position of the eighteen-unit complex. The condo unit came with the job and he only had to pay for utilities.

"How'd you find out about this job? I need to start seriously thinking about what I'm going to do when I leave the factory," Sean said. He sat on the upholstered sofa and stretched his legs out in front of him, crossing them at the ankle. They had lost touch when Dexter joined the army, but reconnected after he retired from the military and returned to Cincinnati. Since then, they'd supported each other through life's many ups and downs.

"Katara's friend lives in the complex and had mentioned they were looking to hire someone for the position. The person who lived here before partied all the time, barely took care of the building."

"So they figured they'd get an old dude to fill the position instead of a young buck," Sean joked, his weathered face stretching into a wide grin.

Dex shook his head and smiled. "I might be getting older, but I don't consider myself old."

"Yeah, that's what everyone pushing sixty says."

Dex didn't feel his age, and at times he wondered where the years had gone. Granted, he had screwed up many of those years with one bad decision after another. Now he had a second chance to get his life back on track, and that's what he intended to do.

"All right, let's get those boxes in here so I can get settled," Dexter said, and grabbed his keys off the granite counter top. "I figured we can unload the truck and set everything over there until I have a chance to unpack." He pointed to a corner of the living room near the bank of windows.

"Sounds good. The sooner we get done, the faster we can get ready for the game tonight. The Cavaliers are playing the Warriors and I know it's going to be a good one."

They headed outside and started carting boxes into the condo. Dexter's unit was on the first floor and he was glad they didn't have to deal with any stairs.

On one of the trips out, he slowed and glanced around his new community. Like him, Over-the-Rhine had once been in bad shape, but had gone through a major transformation. Dexter almost didn't recognize the vibrant area.

Contentment rested in his soul. *I've made it.*

He climbed into the truck and grabbed a large box and a duffel bag that held some of his clothes. This move was the beginning of a new chapter in his life.

After taking the items in, he and Sean walked outside together for the remaining boxes. Sean climbed into the back of the truck and brought several containers to the opening and set them down on the floor of the truck.

Dexter reached for a large bag, but stopped when the hair on the back of his neck lifted. He turned and glanced around the parking lot. The moving truck was parked near the entrance, giving him a good view of most of the lot. At first, he didn't see anything out of the norm, but then he spotted two women near the last row pulling a number of bags from a car.

Well, I'll be damned.

Sean followed Dexter's gaze. "Mmm, nice-looking women. I take it you know them?" He climbed down and stood next to Dexter.

"I only know the one with the curly hair. That's Mona, the woman I was telling you about." Dexter had first met Mona a few months ago at the Jenkins family Sunday brunch.

"*That's* Mona?" Sean asked, disbelief dripping from each word. "There's no way in hell you can pull a woman like that. Man, she is *way* out of your league. I can already tell she has champagne taste, which won't work with your soda-pop budget. Look at her."

Dexter *was* looking. And like the last time he'd seen her, he liked what he saw.

"There's an air of royalty about her. She's practically floating through the lot. Figures you'd fall for a high-society woman, knowing she don't want nothin' to do with your old, country ass."

Dexter chuckled. "Man, shut up."

"When you said you were ready to get back in the game, I had no idea you'd be trying to aim that high."

Dexter studied Mona as she slowly headed toward the door, the other woman walking at her side. Was it too much to hope that Mona lived in the building?

She was as pretty as he remembered. Even at her age, there was an innocence about her that called to him. Her skin, the color of chocolate with a hint of cream, was blemish-free, but it was her mouth that drew his attention. *Those lips.* The raspberry-colored gloss only highlighted for him that she had the prettiest lips he'd ever seen on a woman.

As she moved closer, he took in the whole package. When they had met months ago, she'd been dressed conservatively and seemed shy. Now, though she still seemed a little unsure of herself, the denim outfit hugging her womanly curves hinted at a sensual and exciting woman. Her hair was shorter than the last time he'd seen her, but the long strands still brushed her shoulders with big curls framing her face.

Classy *and* sexy.

Dexter removed his baseball cap and nodded when she was a few steps away. "Hello there, Mona."

A hesitant smile graced her lips. Dexter hadn't been this attracted to a woman in a long time. Not since the day he had met his ex-wife.

"H—Hi, Dexter."

Chapter Two

Mona wasn't good with small talk, and it didn't help that Dexter was looking at her as if she was a juicy steak he had just taken off the grill. He was older than what she'd had in mind when she told her sister she was ready to date. Yet, there was something about him that sent warmth through her from the inside out. He wasn't as good-looking as Russell, but what he lacked in attractiveness, he made up for with a deep baritone that had goosebumps traveling up her arm. He also had a cool, laid-back confident demeanor that intrigued her.

"What are you doing here?" she finally asked. The small moving truck he was standing next to spoke volumes, but she didn't want to assume.

He twisted his baseball cap within his hand. It dawned on her that she didn't meet too many men who practiced proper etiquette and removed their hat when greeting a woman.

"I'm moving in. I'm the new maintenance man for the building."

Mona could've sworn she heard her sister snicker. She didn't dare look at Johnette. Right now, it was taking all she had not to fidget under Dexter's intense gaze.

At least six feet tall and maybe 220 pounds, he was fit, but wasn't necessarily the type of man a woman would take a second or third look at in passing. Except...he did have broad shoulders. And that smile. Goodness. His smile could light up the darkest day and heat the coldest night.

Her gaze traveled a little lower. She suddenly had an urge to sneak her hands beneath his navy-blue T-shirt and run her hands over his wide, muscular chest. He had a physical build of someone half his age.

Mona wasn't sure where that thought came from, but she had to admit it was nice to see that he didn't have a beer belly, like so many men his age.

Her gaze eventually returned to his face. Like when she'd met him months ago at the Jenkins' estate, there was something so alluring about him. Maybe it was his arresting eyes and his easy, friendly smile.

"Since it doesn't seem like my sister is going to introduce us, I'm Johnette Gregory." Johnette shuffled her bags to one hand and shook Dexter's hand.

"Dexter Jenkins. It's a pleasure to meet you. Nick and Sumeera have mentioned you on a number of occasions." Dexter introduced them to his friend Sean before the man left them to carry a few items into the building.

"Johnette, I think I remember Sumeera saying that you had moved to Mexico," Dexter said. "Have you moved back to town or are you visiting?"

A stab of jealousy sliced through Mona. Of course, Sumeera had talked about Johnette. She was more of a mother to Sumeera than Mona could ever hope to be. The two of them even finished each other's sentences, and if Johnette and Mona stood side by side in front of Sumeera, Johnette would be the one she'd address first.

That knowledge was something Mona continued to struggle with. If only she hadn't put Russell's needs before her relationship with Sumeera.

"I'm visiting for a couple of weeks." Mona heard her sister explain. As usual, Johnette kept the conversation flowing smoothly, even joking in that effortless way of hers.

Mona glanced away, half-listening while the two laughed as if they were old friends. As a child, she had always walked in Johnette's shadow. Older by two years, her sister was everything she had hoped to one day be. Independent. Outgoing. Witty. Those were only a few adjectives that best described Johnette back then and now.

"Well, I'll leave you two be," her sister said, giving Mona a little nudge as she took a step closer to the door. "Sis, I'll see you inside. Dexter, it was a pleasure meeting you."

"Same here."

Dexter's gaze immediately returned to Mona and anxiousness swirled in the pit of her stomach. How the heck was she going to get into the dating world if she couldn't even hold a conversation with a man?

"It's good seeing you again," Dexter said.

"You too. I must say, I'm a little surprised you're here."

He explained how he came to get the job as the caretaker of the property and told her which unit he would be living in. She appreciated how comfortable he seemed sharing his personal business. *An open man.* That was something she wasn't accustomed to. Unless Russell was discussing business, he wasn't a sharer of information, especially with people he barely knew.

"How long have you lived in the building?" he asked.

"About three months."

"Do you like the area?"

"I love it. It reminds me a little bit of Greenwich Village in New York."

Mona didn't bother telling him she had chosen the neighborhood in hopes of lighting a fire under her lack of a social life. The area provided numerous restaurants, theaters, and she could take the street car to Findlay Market. She was also within walking distance to anything else she needed, which was good since she didn't own a car. Even having her driver's license, she rarely drove since she'd had a driver at her disposal while living in New York.

They continued their small talk, with Dexter expertly guiding the conversation until a car pulling into the complex's parking lot snagged their attention.

"Forgive my manners," Dexter said. "I've kept you out here and I bet those bags are getting heavy. May I carry them in for you?"

"Oh no, that's…" Mona started, but caught herself. He was clearly interested if his steady gaze, easy smile, and the effort he'd put into getting her to talk with him was any indication. Besides, if he wanted to be a gentleman, who was she to stop him? "Sure, that would be nice."

As he grabbed hold of all of the bags, his friend returned to the truck.

"Sean, I'll be right back."

Sean flashed a schoolboy grin and chuckled. Mona's face heated at the knowing look Dexter's friend gave them. She suddenly felt like that awkward teenager back in high school.

"No problem," Sean said, and walked up the ramp of the moving truck. "It was nice meeting you, Mona. Hope to see you again sometime."

Mona smiled. "Same here."

With the handles of the bags in one large hand, Dexter directed her inside. His free hand at the small of her back sent an exciting tingle shooting up her spine.

God. When was the last time a simple touch sent butterflies fluttering in her stomach?

Dexter followed close as she walked up the stairs to the second floor and headed down the hall.

"I'm the last door on the left." Mona dug her keys out of her pocket. She was glad she had given Johnette a spare set the day before. Otherwise, Mona might not have had the chance to talk with Dexter alone. They hadn't been outside long, but long enough for her to think that he was a nice guy.

"Would you like to go out for dinner with me Friday night?" Caught by surprise, Mona's brows shot up. Before

13

she could respond, he continued. "I know you don't know me, but if you ask your son-in-law, he'll tell you I'm a stand-up guy. I'd love to get to know you better and maybe introduce you to a couple of hot spots in the area."

Mona glanced away, folding her bottom lip between her teeth. Nick wouldn't have introduced them in the first place if Dexter wasn't a decent man, but still. Though she wanted to say yes, something kept her from opening her mouth. Despite what she had told her sister about wanting to start dating and having some fun, Dexter wasn't what she had in mind. He seemed like a nice guy, but...

"Don't say no." He interrupted her thoughts. "I guarantee you'll have a good time."

Mona couldn't stop a smile from creeping across her lips. "Guarantee? You sound pretty confident, Mr. Jenkins."

Dexter laughed, and the melodious sound sent a flutter of delight shooting through her.

"You'll soon learn that I'm a man of my word, Ms. Gregory. So, what do you say? Wanna go out on the town with me Friday night?"

She smiled. *Oh, what the heck.*

"I'd love to."

*

"I'm guessing by that goofy grin on your face, the conversation with Ms. Mona went well," Sean said when Dexter met him at the door of the building. He grabbed one of the last two boxes from his friend and they headed for Dexter's unit.

"I have a date for Friday night," he said.

Sean grinned. "Damn, man. You didn't waste any time."

Honestly, Dexter hadn't planned to ask her out at that moment, but there was just something about her. He couldn't explain the immediate attraction. Granted, she was a stunning woman. But there was something deep inside of him that had been drawn to her from the moment their gazes collided that Sunday at the brunch. Today was no different. If anything, that unexplainable feeling had been even more intense.

"Asking her out must mean you're finally moving on from Lillie," Sean said, speaking of Dexter's ex-wife. He added the box he was carrying to the pile they'd already brought in. "'Bout time you stopped pining over her. The woman has moved on."

"I'm not pining over her. I've accepted that she's remarried and I'm happy for her. We're still good friends, and we talk occasionally. It's just that usually after we talk, I start to reevaluate my own life. You're right. She's moved on. It's time I did, too."

"And that's exactly what you're doing."

Dexter grabbed a couple of bottles of water from the refrigerator and handed one to Sean.

"Thanks." His friend removed the top and took a long swig of the cold liquid before wiping his mouth with the back of his hand. "You have definitely stepped up your game getting out on your own and moving into this place. Maybe your life is turning around."

"I hope so." Dexter finished his water and set the empty container on the counter. "I'm ready to settle down, get married, and live the second half of my life with a wonderful woman."

His ex-wife Lillie had been the perfect wife. A great cook, excellent mother, and she loved him unconditionally. Shame he couldn't get his act together in time to save his marriage, making one mistake after another. She deserved happiness, and had found love and now lived in Florida with her husband.

"You're a better man than me. After splitting with my ex, the last thing I want is to go down that marriage road again."

Dexter understood his friend's sentiment. Unlike Sean, he was a traditional guy who believed a man was better off with a wife. Despite how things turned out between him and Lillie, he loved being married.

So many mistakes.

Dexter drew in a breath as guilt lodged in his chest. It had taken him years to believe he was worthy of a second chance at love. He'd had the best life a man could have, but let it slip through his fingers.

Sean clapped his hand on Dexter's shoulder and squeezed. "Another go-around at marriage might not be for me, but I could see you tying the knot again. You always were a glutton for punishment."

Dexter shook his head and laughed. Maybe he was, but he had experienced more joy than pain. He planned to make sure the rest of his years on earth were even better than the earlier ones.

"Where are you planning to take Mona?"

"I'm not sure yet, but I promised her a good time."

"Somehow, my friend, I have a feeling that a good time to you might be different than a good time to her."

Dexter couldn't argue with him there. It didn't take much for Dexter to have a nice time. Eating a burger while watching a basketball game, especially if his team was winning, meant a fun evening for him. Maybe he should've asked Mona what she enjoyed doing.

He smiled to himself. Good thing he thought to get her telephone number before he left her at her door. Now he had an excuse to give her a call before their date. He had a feeling he only had one shot with the shy beauty before she moved on to the next guy.

I need to make sure this is the best date she ever had.

"Are you going to tell her about...your past?"

Dexter released an uneasy sigh. "Maybe."

Having to discuss some aspects of his past with any woman he decided to get serious with wasn't going to be easy. He'd have to play it by ear.

Hopefully this wouldn't be his last date with her.

Chapter Three

What was I thinking saying yes to a date?

Mona put the finishing touches on her makeup and fluffed her curls. That question had played over and over in her head for the last few days. At first, she'd been excited, though a little nervous, that a man even wanted to take her out. Now, days later, reality had set in. She wasn't sure she was ready for this next step. If canceling for no good reason at the last minute wasn't so tacky, she would call Dexter and do just that.

Who dated at her age?

What would they even talk about?

She'd been kidding herself when she told Johnette she was ready to live a little, have a fling or two. Mona wanted to believe she could be fun and carefree, but now she wasn't sure she could pull it off. Russell might not have been her first boyfriend, but she could count on three fingers the number of guys she'd ever gone out with.

She shook her head.

Don't think about that. New day. New attitude.

She had to keep reminding herself she wasn't the same person. No way was she going to let her age and lack of experience stop her from living her best life.

"This second half is going to be better than my first half."

She smiled, feeling encouraged. Finding some friends was her first order of business.

"Might as well start with Dexter."

After one last look in the bathroom mirror, she stepped into the bedroom, grabbed her handbag and exited the room.

"Don't you have something more casual you can wear?" Johnette asked the moment Mona strolled into the living room, giving her outfit a critical inspection. "You look like somebody's matronly mother heading out to church."

Mona huffed. "I *am* somebody's matronly mother; and grandmother, for that matter."

"Yeah, but you don't have to look like it. That blouse is beautiful if you're going to high tea or modeling for a fashion magazine, and that skirt is cute, but it's too long...and stiff. All you're missing is one of those wide-brimmed hats women wear to church, and you would look like a missionary." She laughed and Mona rolled her eyes. Johnette had always been a straight shooter, saying whatever came to mind. Right now, Mona could do without her tactless comments.

"I think this is perfectly fine to wear for an evening out with a man."

"Dexter told you to dress casual. That's not casual, Mona. Besides, if you're going to wear a skirt, heck, at least show a little leg. And what was the point of us going shopping the other day if you're not going to wear the outfits you purchased?" Johnette didn't wait for a response. She marched passed Mona and headed for the master bedroom.

"I know how to dress." Mona stood in the doorway of her bedroom, her hands on her hips as her sister rummaged through the closet. "I've been dressing myself for years."

"I'll admit, you do know how to dress...for a person living in New York or Paris. You're in Cincinnati now. Try to fit in," came Johnette's muffled response.

Seconds later, she stood in the middle of the room holding up two potential outfits. One was a light-blue fitted sweater with a V-neck that dipped a little lower than Mona usually preferred, and she paired it with winter-white pants. The other outfit was a white tunic with bell sleeves and a hemline longer on one side. She paired it with skinny black pants.

"You say you want to be this sophisticated single woman who just wants to have fun. It's time you started looking like one. Personally, I'd go with this one." She held up the blue sweater. "It's chic and sexy without looking slutty. Oh, and wear some higher heels. Dexter is tall. Might as well show off a pair of those overpriced wedge heels."

Mona studied the clothes before glancing at the outfit she had on. An outfit she had only worn once to a charity breakfast months ago.

"Fine. Maybe you're right. Now get out of my room."

Johnette laughed. "*Fine.*"

Mona couldn't help but smile. How many times had Johnette kicked her out of her bedroom when they were growing up? The last few days together had been wonderful, reminding her of their high school years. Seemed like a lifetime ago, but it also seemed like yesterday, if that made any sense.

"Hurry it up. Dexter will probably be here soon. Oh, and wear silver jewelry. Not those overpriced diamonds dripping from your ears and around your neck." With that, she was gone.

Mona stared at herself in the full-length mirror and grudgingly agreed with her sister. She did look as if she was going to a formal tea party instead of on a date.

As she quickly changed clothes, she thought about how Johnette would be heading back to Mexico in less than a week. Mona already knew she was going to miss her. The past few days had been fun, and she couldn't remember the last time she had actually thought of a day as fun. How sad was that?

Now more than ever she needed to make some friends. A daunting task she wasn't looking forward to.

19

She hurried and slipped into a pair of off-white wedge heels. Seeing herself in the mirror, she couldn't help but smile. The outfit was perfect.

Her phone buzzed and she dug it out of her handbag. Glancing at the screen, she didn't recognize the number, but thought that maybe it was Dexter. She hoped he wasn't canceling.

"Hello."

"Hello, love," the familiar voice said, stopping her in her tracks.

"*Russell?* How did you get this number?"

He chuckled as if she'd said something funny. "Love, you have to do better than getting another phone to keep me from finding you. What I want to know is why you changed your number?"

If Russell had her telephone number, chances were he knew where she lived. It's not like Mona feared him. He had never threatened her life, but those last months together had her believing he needed psychological help. The mood swings. The delusional thoughts. Anxious one minute and depressed the next. At first, the changes were subtle. But when he and Nick fought because of the way Russell had manhandled Sumeera, Mona was convinced he needed help. Help she couldn't give him. It was then she made up her mind to leave him.

"Russell, why are you calling? We agreed it was time we went our separate ways."

"I didn't agree to any such thing. Your home is here in New York. I know you want to get to know our daughter better, but don't you think it's time for you to come home now? It's been three weeks."

"Russell, I've been here for six months."

Silence filled the phone line. This was another sign something was going on with his mind.

"I know. I'm just…I miss you. I get it now, Mona. I've taken you for granted and I'm sorry. Come home and I'll make it up to you."

"We talked about this months ago. I live in Cincinnati now. Did you contact that doctor I recommended?"

"I don't need a damn doctor, especially not some quack!" Anger rang through his voice. "I forget things sometimes or have a bad day occasionally. Everyone does."

"Not like you've been doing lately. You need to get help and sooner rather than later."

"You sound like you care. If my health is so important to you, come home and let's go see the doctor together."

Johnette knocked on Mona's bedroom door. "Hurry up, sis. Dexter will be here soon and I want to see what you look like."

Mona cover the phone with her hand. "Be right there," she called out. "Russell, I have to go. Please call that doctor."

"I can send a plane for you. Will you be able to come home in the next few days?"

Mona closed her eyes and rubbed her forehead. There was no reasoning with him. She might not love him like she once had, but she would always care about him. But Mona didn't know what else to do to make him see reason.

"You're not listening to me, Russell. You need help and I'm staying in Cincinnati." A thought popped into her mind. Of course he hadn't called the therapist. She'd been the one who made all of his dental and doctor appointments through the years. Had it not been for her, there was no telling if he would have ever taken care of his health while they were together. "You know what I'm going to do, Russell?"

"I hope you're going to tell me you're coming home."

"No, but tomorrow I'll call and make arrangements for you. Then I'll let you know the date and time, but you have to keep the appointment." And she needed to learn how to stop feeling responsible for him.

He released an irritated groan and said, "Just come home. We can discuss this when you get here. I promise—"

"Goodbye, Russell." Mona disconnected, frustrated with herself. She couldn't help someone who wasn't willing to help himself. That was one of her problems. They'd been together for so long, she cared about his well-being, especially since he didn't have anyone else.

Guilt snuck up on her from time to time regarding the way she had up and left. Granted, she'd talked about leaving for years, but he would always talk her out of it and assumed they'd be together forever.

"I need to start focusing on me," she mumbled into the quietness of the room.

She shoved her cell phone into the handbag and it rang just as she reached the bedroom door. A quick glance at the screen revealed it was Russell. No doubt he would call again, but she didn't have time for his antics right now.

"Okay, I'm ready," Mona said when she walked back into the living room, feeling like a new woman. The right outfit could change a woman's attitude, but she had forgotten how much it made a difference.

"Now *that's* what I'm talking about," Johnette said.

"I can't believe I'm saying this, but you were right."

Her sister stood from the sofa. "I'm always right. But I'm not going to always be here. If you want to be this new and improved person you've been talking about, it's going to be up to you to start looking the part."

Before Johnette could continue with her speech, a knock sounded on the door.

Mona's pulse amped up and her breathing increased.

"Okay, I'm going into the guest room until you guys leave. And Mona, don't overthink everything. Try to have fun." Johnette hugged her and scurried off to the bedroom.

Okay, here goes.

*

Hot damn, Dexter thought when Mona's door swung open. All he could do was stare at the vision before him. If he thought she was stunning before, tonight she was absolutely gorgeous. He was glad he had opted for a sweater and dress pants. Had he gone with the long-sleeved T-shirt and jeans, he would've been sorely underdressed.

Sean had been right about one thing. Mona did look like money.

"Hi," he finally said, feeling like a bonehead for just staring at her.

Her smile widened and his heart almost stopped. Those pretty lips were going to be the death of him. He was such a goner.

"You're right on time. Come in. Let me grab my purse."

Dexter watched her walk away. The gentle sway of her hips—left, right, left—was almost hypnotic. She wasn't skinny or fat, but had a shapely body like a woman half her age.

"Do you think I'll need a jacket?" Mona asked when she suddenly turned to face him, no doubt catching him staring at her butt.

Dexter's gaze snapped up and slammed into hers, concern on her face.

She's going to think I'm a pervert if I don't get myself together.

"I'm sorry. What did you say?"

"Are you okay?" she asked and approached him. "If you don't want to go out, I—"

"Oh no. I'm fine. What did you ask me?"

"I asked if I needed a jacket."

"It's not too bad outside, but I'm sure it's going to get a little cooler. It's probably a good idea to bring one."

Dexter stood near the door and glanced around her living space, taking it in for the first time since arriving. The layout was the same as his, but it definitely had a woman's touch. A woman's expensive touch. From what he could see, the kitchen, dining room, and living room all looked as if the space was lifted from *House Beautiful* magazine. There was a lot of white, including the sofa and the carpet. Her accent colors were gray and splashes of navy blue. She definitely had an eye for interior design.

"Okay, I think I'm ready."

"You look beautiful. I'm going to be the envy of every man out tonight."

Her smile was shy. "Thank you."

"Nice place you have here," he said, and reached for the door knob.

"Thanks. I feel like I'm finally settled in."

They headed toward the front entrance, Dexter's hand at the small of her back. He couldn't help wanting to touch her. Hell, he actually wanted to bury his face against her scented skin. When he held the door for her, the scent of gardenias wafted to his nose as she passed him. He sucked in a breath, inhaling her enticing fragrance, before releasing the breath slowly.

She was tempting and smelled good. He had a feeling it was going to be a great night.

"Where are we going?" Mona asked when they stepped outside.

Dexter glanced down at her feet and her high heels. "How comfortable are your shoes?"

"They're actually a lot more comfortable than they look. Why do you ask?"

"I was thinking we can walk to the restaurant. If you're up for it."

There was that heart-stopping smile again. "That would be nice. I moved to the condo because I liked the area, but I haven't taken the opportunity to really explore."

"Excellent. I was thinking after dinner we can head to a little jazz club a friend of mine recently opened. They play R&B oldies on Friday nights. Hopefully, you like dancing."

Mona gave a nervous laugh, her eyes sparkling with delight. "I haven't danced in years, but that sounds like fun."

"I'm glad you think so. I guaranteed you a good time tonight, and I plan to deliver."

Chapter Four

Giddiness replaced Mona's earlier nervousness as Dexter held her hand and they strolled past Washington Park's performance stage. The moment felt so natural, as if they'd done this many times before. Though she tried not reading too much into the hand-holding, she had to admit the intimacy of his touch felt nice. Tender moments were rare in her previous relationship.

Russell did an outstanding job providing any material item she could dream of, and for the most part, he was kind to her. Their early years together were fun and adventurous, but as the business grew, the passion between them slowly declined. Sadly, she couldn't remember the last time he'd held her hand or hugged her close. Already Dexter was proving to be…

Mona halted the route of her thoughts. She had vowed not to compare any man she met to her ex. More importantly, she had promised herself she wouldn't waste any brain power on Russell tonight. It would've been easier had he not called before she left home.

"You doin' okay?" Dexter asked, squeezing her hand and effectively pulling her back to the present. "I probably should've re-thought the idea of walking, considering the heels you're wearing."

She smiled up at him. If only he knew how good she felt, how happy she was at that very moment. It wasn't because it was a perfect spring night. No. Her joy had everything to do with his company.

"I'm great. I'm glad you suggested we walk. It's a beautiful night." The weather was comfortable with a cool breeze kissing her cheek ever so gently.

Dexter went back to giving her some history on the Over-the-Rhine area as they passed one charming ornate brick building after another.

"Tens of millions of dollars went into revitalizing the community. It was only a few years ago that the area was deemed one of the most dangerous neighborhoods in the country. You definitely wouldn't have wanted to be around here at night. Now, it's almost unrecognizable."

"Sumeera told me the same thing when she first brought me here to tour a few condos for sale."

As a real estate agent, her daughter was knowledgeable about the city she had spent most of her life in. They'd visited a number of neighborhoods, but after touring three condominiums in the area, Mona had decided this was where she wanted to be.

"People who used to live in the suburbs slowly started moving back to the city, and before long, shops and restaurants started popping up," Dexter continued.

She could listen to his deep baritone all day, every day. Not because he knew so much about the area and the historical architecture. Even describing the neighborhood, he made it sound sexy. His voice, a velvety rumble, sent tingles through her body. It had been a long time since she'd felt tingles anywhere.

Mona couldn't have asked for a better way to start a first date. When she'd answered her door minutes ago, she'd been pleasantly surprised at how nice he looked. The four-button mock-neck sweater was light gray, and he'd paired it with a pair of black tailored slacks. Seeing him the other day in T-shirts and jeans, she hadn't known what to expect. He cleaned up nice. And more importantly, she was comfortable with him. Already this was turning into one of the most romantic dates she'd ever been on.

Dexter held her hand tighter as they sidestepped groups of people lined up on the sidewalk in front of a theater. They kept moving down Vine Street toward a number of restaurants.

"We're almost there. I hope you like pizza."

Mona chuckled. She hadn't had pizza in years, preferring healthier options, but instead of telling him that, she said, "I do."

They crossed the street and a short while later, they strolled into a cozy bistro. The smell of fresh-baked bread, garlic, onions, and oregano greeted them at the door. Mona's stomach growled in anticipation. The eatery was a perfect blend of romantic—with the dimmed lights and candles on each table—and relaxing, with a laid-back vibe.

Within minutes they were directed to a small table for two covered with a red and white tablecloth.

"Is this okay?" Dexter asked, pulling the chair out for her.

Sweet, with a sexy voice, and he's a gentleman.

Oh yeah, Mona could definitely get used to this type of attention.

"This is fine. Thank you."

"Welcome. Can I get you something to drink, maybe a glass of Chianti or Zinfandel?" a server asked, placing two small drink napkins on the table.

"A glass of Chianti sounds good," Mona said, and glanced at the menu.

"And you, sir?"

"Just water for me. Thank you," Dexter responded, which made Mona look up. Very few people she knew had dinner without a glass of wine.

Small talk flowed easily between them after they placed their order. Her first impression of him, when they initially met, had been turned on its heel when he started talking about the environment and global warming. Dexter was a good example of a man who shouldn't be judged by his appearance. He seemed to know something about everything.

The server returned with a thin-crust medium cheese, sausage and mushroom pizza, two side salads, and an order of garlic bread.

"All right, Mona. Tell me something about yourself that I don't know."

*

Dexter had wanted to ask a few personal questions during their walk to the restaurant, but thought better of it. When they left the condo, she seemed nervous. He figured discussing safe topics, like the weather and the neighborhood, would help loosen her up. Now that they were in a relaxed environment, he wanted to know everything about the conservative beauty sitting across from him.

"Well, my real name is Mona Lisa Gregory, though I usually go by Mona. And I'm old enough to have a 35-year-old daughter," she said, smiling, and Dexter chuckled. His gaze went immediately to those pretty heart-shaped lips. He couldn't help wondering if they were as soft as they looked.

"Mona Lisa, huh? That's a beautiful name for a beautiful woman."

"Thank you, but I *hated it* growing up," she blurted and then laughed, but quickly covered her mouth with her hand. "Sorry, I didn't mean to be so loud, but back then, kids teased me relentlessly. Now I rarely share my full name."

"Well, I'm honored you deem me worthy of sharing your…secret with me."

She smiled. "You have a way about you that makes me feel at ease."

"I'm glad to hear that."

Dexter's gaze dropped down to where she was using her knife and fork to eat her pizza. He fought a smile. This was a first. Never in his sixty years had he seen anyone eat pizza with a fork. The gesture fit her prim and proper demeanor. Everything about the woman was cute, delicate, and enticing.

He lifted his slice, folded it and savored the enticing scent before taking a large bite. Cheese with mushrooms and sauce dripped, but he caught them with his finger stuffing them into his mouth, not wanting to waste a single bite. He didn't care that he wasn't practicing good manners. Pizza wasn't meant to be eaten with proper etiquette.

The delectable spices burst inside his mouth and he moaned internally. There was nothing like a good slice of pizza to make up for a long, exhausting week. He'd been looking forward to the night from the moment he'd asked her out, and this was worth the wait. Great company and amazing food. What more could a guy ask for?

He glanced over to find Mona staring at him in awe.

"Clearly, I'm doing this all wrong," she said with a laugh.

"*Clearly*," Dexter cracked and wiped his mouth. "For the record, pizza is meant to be messy and eaten as such. Lose the fork and knife. I guarantee your slice will taste a thousand percent better."

She followed his lead as he showed her the proper steps to eating a thin-sliced pizza. Where he held his moan in, Mona released hers and closed her eyes in the process.

Her seductive sighs filled Dexter's ears, raked up his spine, and sent a tantalizing shiver through his body.

Well, damn. She had taken his love of pizza to a different level. He would never eat another slice again without remembering this night. If she enjoyed it with that much passion, he could only imagine what she'd be like between the sheets.

Okay, buddy. Don't go there. Yet.

"Oh my goodness. You were right. This is *amazing*," she said, as if it was the first time she'd eaten a slice of pizza. She dabbed at the corners of her mouth and smiled up at him. "Thank you."

Dexter swallowed hard. "No. Thank you," he mumbled, tugging on the leg of his pants and discreetly moving around on his chair. His shaft pressed uncomfortably against his zipper, and he tried to think of less pleasant things than getting her into bed. It had been awhile for him and if watching her eat pizza had him hard, he didn't even want to imagine how it was going to be the first time he tasted her gorgeous mouth.

"What else don't I know about you?" he finally asked after a long moment.

"My favorite thing in the world these days is spending time with my granddaughter." Love shone in her eyes and he recalled the birth of his first grandchild.

"I can understand that. Chanelle is a cutie, but I see good looks run in the family."

Mona lowered her eyes and smiled, color tinting her cheeks. Dexter already knew making her blush was going to be one of his new favorite things to do.

"And that daughter of yours definitely found herself a good guy," Dexter said of his younger cousin, Nick, Mona's son-in-law.

"I have to agree. He's the best. Actually, the whole Jenkins family have been wonderful. Soon after I moved to Cincinnati, they embraced me as if they had known me all their lives." Mona took a small bite of garlic bread and wiped her mouth. "Now, how are you related?"

"Steven Jenkins, Nick's grandfather, is my first cousin. As a kid, I always looked up to him and he took me under his wing when I was a teenager."

Even back then, Steven had a good head on his shoulders and had vowed to be a millionaire one day. He had accomplished that years ago with Jenkins & Sons Construction.

"The Jenkins family is one of the largest families I've ever been around," Mona said. "It's fascinating to see them spend so much time together and to witness how close everyone is."

Dexter nodded, knowing she was referring to how Steven and Katherine hosted Sunday brunch every week. They expected their children and grandchildren to show up.

"Yeah, Steven's parents had a ton of children. That's probably why he and Katherine wanted a large family. I think they have at least seven kids and even more grandkids. It's getting hard to keep up with everyone."

"And now they have great-great-grands," Mona added. "What about you? Do you have brothers and sisters?"

"Yes. My family isn't as big. I have two older brothers and two sisters."

"You're the baby?"

Dexter laughed. "I haven't been called that in over fifty years, but yes, I'm the youngest of five. None of them live in town. Some are in Georgia and the others are in Florida."

"What about children? Have you ever been married?"

"Yes, to both. I was married for over thirty years before my divorce. We have two great kids, a girl and a boy. My daughter, Katara, is thirty-four, lives here, and is married with two children. My son, Dexter Jr., is thirty, lives in Florida with his wife and one child."

They continued eating and talking about their children and grandchildren. Dexter had already known that Sumeera had been raised by Johnette for much of her life. But it surprised him at Mona's reasons for sending her only child to live with her sister. In his world, mothers would give up a limb before leaving their child to be raised by someone else.

"Letting my daughter live away from me all of those years is my biggest…well, one of my biggest regrets. Don't get me wrong, Johnette did a wonderful job with Sumeera. I just wished I hadn't been so focused on her father and growing his property development business. If I could do that part of my life over again, I would."

On the table, Dexter covered her hand with his. "We all have things in our past we wish we could change." God knows he did.

"Thank you." Mona eased her hand from his and released a shaky sigh. "I'm glad Sumeera has forgiven me. Our relationship is growing stronger by the day."

Dexter nodded, trying not to think too hard about his own past. He had hurt a number of people through the years and had finally mended those relationships.

"Do you keep in contact with your ex-husband?"

Mona sipped from her glass of wine, glancing at him over the rim before slowly setting the glass on the table.

"I've never been married."

Dexter's hand stalled on a slice of pizza and he struggled to keep his jaw from dropping. How was it possible she hadn't married the man she'd been with longer than most marriages last? Where he came from, if you're willing and in love with a person for so many years, you married them.

"We were together until recently, but we just..." She shrugged. "We just never got married."

"Was that by choice?"

Her gaze shot up and zoned in on him. They stared into each other's eyes for a long beat, and Dexter waited impatiently for her to respond.

"No. There was a time I wanted to get married and have more children, but that's not what Russell wanted."

Dexter studied her for a long time as she went back to eating. So far, she was nothing like he expected.

"Do you think you'll ever get married? Is that something you still want?" he asked.

"No. I'm over the whole holy matrimony-'til-death-do-us-part shenanigans. It wasn't meant to be, and I've moved on."

Dexter dropped back against his seat. He wasn't buying it. She wasn't the type who enjoyed being single and alone. Or maybe that's what he wanted to believe about her. He planned to spend the remainder of his life married and in a loving relationship. Apparently, that's not what she wanted for her life. Then again...

"What does 'it wasn't meant to be and I've moved on' mean, exactly?"

"It means I sacrificed everything dear to me—for a man. I'm not doing that again. I've moved on from him, and my daughter is grown and has a beautiful family. It's my turn to start enjoying life and do some of the things I've wanted to do."

Dexter nodded, listening to what she was saying and trying to interpret what wasn't being said.

"As for my personal life, I plan to date some. I'd love to meet more people, but I'm not interested in being in a committed relationship."

Dexter wasn't sure how to respond. Their future goals didn't line up. Yet, there was still something about the woman that called to him, a strong magnetic pull he couldn't explain. The sensation had only been experienced one other time, shortly before he'd asked Lillie to marry him. He didn't have an explanation for the feeling but many in the family claimed that when a Jenkins man identified his future wife, he just knew.

It was too early for him to even be thinking about anything long-term with Mona, but rarely did he ignore a gut feeling.

"What about you? Why aren't you still married?" Mona asked, cutting into his thoughts.

"I had a wonderful marriage until I screwed it up with one bad decision after another. Couldn't get my act together fast enough to keep my wife from walking away."

He hadn't dated seriously since Lillie. He'd taken women to dinner, but none of those instances led to anything more than a friendly outing. Until a few years ago, he was still learning how to love himself after making such a mess of his life.

"I don't think God meant for man to be on this earth alone. Now that my life is in order, if the right woman comes along, I plan to get married again someday."

"Really? You'd try it again...at your age?"

Dexter laughed. "I'm not *that* old, and I'm not dead."

"Sorry. That didn't come out right," she said sheepishly.

Dexter waved her off, finding it cute how horrified she looked after speaking the words.

"I still have things I want to do, and I have a lot to offer a woman. I can do everything I used to do. I can't go as long, but I can still hold my own," he said, making sure to maintain eye contact to ensure she understood what he was saying. Unlike many people his age, he wasn't on any medication and was in the best shape of his life.

After a slight hesitation, her lips parted in surprise. "*Ohhh*. I see. Um…good to know." She glanced down at her lap nervously and after a moment, lifted her gaze to him. "What were some of the mistakes you made in your marriage?" When Dexter didn't respond right away, she added, "If it's too personal, you don't have to answer."

"No, I don't mind. We came out tonight to get to know each other better. I might not be proud of some aspects of my past, but I understand those decisions and experiences together make up the person I am today. And to answer your question, I had a drinking problem toward the end of my marriage. I'm an alcoholic."

Chapter Five

Mona tried to control her reaction, but knew she was failing miserably. Heat rose to her cheeks as he looked at her expectantly. That admission wasn't what she expected to hear. She assumed his marriage ended for the same reason so many others end. Cheating.

As for him being an alcoholic, she didn't know anyone who admitted to being an alcoholic and she wasn't sure how to respond.

"Actually, I'm a recovering alcoholic," he added, as if reading her mind. "I've been sober for five years now."

She could hear the pride in his tone and rightfully so. Fighting any addiction wasn't easy and to be sober for that long was definitely something to be proud of. Still, she was at a loss for words.

"Sorry to spring that on you like that. I can assure you I'm harmless, but I speak my mind and I'm always honest."

Mona nodded. "I can appreciate that. My apologies for my reaction. You just caught me off guard."

"I'm sure. This…" he paused, trying to find the right word, "…disease is not something I take lightly. I've learned to manage it. Unfortunately, I didn't get clean in time to save my marriage."

"Oh, Dexter. I'm so sorry."

He opened his mouth, as if planning to say more, but quickly closed it. And for the first time that evening, he didn't look her in the eye. His attention was on everything else around them. When he did finally look at her, the sadness in his eyes almost broke her heart.

One of his hands rested on the table and she placed her hand on top of his.

He glanced down, but didn't say or do anything for the longest time. Eventually, he turned his hand over and held hers tightly. She would be the first to admit that each time she was in his presence, there was an electric sizzle that passed between them. But right now, that powerful force was more potent than ever.

Their gazes met.

Apparently, he felt that inexplicable energy, too.

Mona smiled and eased her hand from his, placing it back in her lap. She had spent most of her life with Russell, and had never felt anything that remotely matched what had just passed between her and Dexter. Then again, maybe she was reading too much into…into whatever this was.

"So, um, what do you do for a living?" she finally asked, at a loss for anything else to say. They were having a great time, and she didn't want his admission and the awkwardness of the subject to overshadow the wonderful evening.

"Well, I retired from the army after twenty years, and then worked at Jenkins & Sons Construction for many years."

"Oh, I didn't realize you worked at the family's construction company."

He nodded. "I used to. Now I live off of my pension. I also have a small handyman business, and I'm the property caretaker at the condominium. What about you? What do you have going on?"

"Well…right now I'm still getting settled," she said, not comfortable in telling him she was living off of a hefty savings account. "But I'm hoping to one day open up a fashion boutique."

He smiled for the first time in the last fifteen minutes, and his whole face lit up. "That's excellent. Do you think you'll open it in this area?"

Dexter rattled off one question after another, and Mona grew even more excited about the venture. Granted, she was in the early stages of her business plan, but she had more ideas than she knew what to do with. She had changed her mind about working in retail. Instead, she'd move forward in opening the boutique and hire someone with experience to run the day-to-day operations.

Sharing some of her initial ideas with Dexter, and hearing his thoughts, suggestions, and even encouragement gave her insight into his entrepreneurial knowledge. Johnette had seemed happy about the idea, but for Dexter to show an interest—and he didn't even know her—said a lot about his character.

They talked while finishing their meal, jumping from one subject to another as if they'd known each other for years. Though Mona had more questions about his marriage, she kept them to herself. This was a first date. Maybe as time went on, she'd learn more about him.

The server set the black folder holding the bill on the table. "No hurry, you can take care of this whenever you're ready."

Dexter glanced at his watch and then opened the folder. He pulled out his wallet and paid the bill. "Are you ready for the second half of our date?"

"Yes, I am."

"Let's go."

A short while later, they arrived at the club as another couple entered.

Mona pulled up short, her lower lip twisted between her teeth.

"What is it?" Dexter asked, his arm around her and his hand resting on her hip.

"Are you sure about this? Are you supposed to go to places like this since…with your…" Her words trailed off and Dexter understood. He moved them to the side of the entrance to let others enter the building.

"Sweetheart, I appreciate you looking out for me, but I have no intention of drinking—ever. So you can put that out of your beautiful head. I have lost everything I once held dear, and have finally made peace with my family and myself. There's no way I'm going back down that road.

"I come here occasionally to listen to music and do a little dancing. Nothing else. I thought you might enjoy it too, but if you would prefer to go somewhere else or call it a night, we—"

She gripped his arm and shook her head. "No. If you're okay being here, then I would love to join you."

"Well, all right then. Let's get this party started. So…do you dance?"

*

Telling Mona about his drinking problem should've felt like a load off his chest, but instead guilt weighed Dexter down. In his heart he was ready to date, but sharing pieces of his past with strangers wasn't going to be easy. The hard part was determining how much to tell.

His AA sponsor had told him he'd know when the time was right and what to share about his past. Dexter wasn't so sure that was true. He wanted Mona to know everything about him, because he felt something for her that he hadn't felt in a long time. He wasn't a fan of secrets. But on the other hand, he never wanted people to look at him the way she had toward the end of their dinner.

In her defense, she handled the news as well as expected. She'd had a few questions, but not as many as she could've asked. There was a moment she had started to ask something else. He wasn't sure what she had seen on his face, but whatever it was kept her from asking anything more. The present guilt he was feeling was because he hadn't told her everything, even though he wanted to.

Dexter guided her into the small club, determine to shake the melancholy trying to pull him under. He wasn't letting his past indiscretions and guilt mess up the rest of their evening.

He glanced around, moving slowly through the dimly lit space in search of a table. He rarely sat at the bar that was on the far side of the room, which was a good thing since there didn't seem to be any seats over there. He hoped to get a little closer to the small stage area where a four-piece band was set up.

Dexter kept a firm grip on Mona's hand as he nodded at a few people he'd seen there before. He spotted a couple vacating a small round table not too far from the makeshift dance floor and headed that way. It was closer to one of the large speakers than he would've preferred, but their choices were limited, especially since people were starting to pour into the quaint establishment.

He placed his hand on the back of one of the chairs before pulling it out. "Is this okay?" he asked close to Mona's ear.

She nodded. No sooner than Dexter sat in the chair next to her, a server approached the table.

"What can I ge…oh hey, Dex," Trina said, once she recognized him. She gave him a one-armed hug and smiled. "Good seeing you." The petite redhead had been working part-time for his friend for years at a different location while she attended college.

"It's good seeing you too, Trina. This is my friend, Mona." The women greeted each other, and Trina and Dexter exchanged small talk while Mona glanced at the drink menu.

"Okay, what can I get you guys?"

Mona frowned as she leaned the menu close to the small lamp that was barely illuminating the table. "Do you have anything without alcohol that isn't soda?"

"We sure do."

Dexter studied Mona as Trina listed non-alcoholic options. He appreciated her willingness to forego alcohol, but he wasn't sure how he felt about her doing it because of him.

She not only hadn't finished her wine earlier, but had moved the glass away from him. He hadn't taken offense, but he didn't want her treating him any different.

Trina turned to him. "What about you? Your usual?"

"Yep, a club soda would be great." Dexter waited until she left the table before addressing the drink issue. "Mona, just because I abstain from alcohol doesn't mean you have to. I'd never ask that of you."

She leaned forward. "I won't pretend I know much about alcoholism, but I respect the journey you have made to stay sober. When I do have a drink, it's usually wine, and only occasionally. So it's no hardship for me to skip it."

"Thank you. That means a lot to me." He had ended many relationships during his recovery for fear of falling back into bad habits. Though he'd had a great support system over the years, he looked forward to building new relationships and hoped Mona would be one of those.

They talked and laughed over their drinks and once again Dexter was amazed at how effortlessly their conversation flowed. Granted the facility wasn't the best place to converse, considering how loud the music was, but it did give him a chance to be close to her. They had to lean in to hear each other.

"Come on. Let's dance." Dexter stood and reached for Mona's hand, but she didn't move. She glanced at the dance floor, her gaze wary.

"I don't know, Dex. It's been so long. The last thing I want to do is crush your feet and embarrass the both of us."

Dexter laughed and tugged her out of her seat. "You're so petite, I doubt you'll crush my size twelves. As for embarrassing me, at my age, there's not much that can embarrass me. Tonight is about us having a good time. Let's not worry about anyone else or what they think of us. Come on. Let's go out here and cut a rug."

Mona laughed, the sound throaty and sexy. Dexter decided to make it his mission to keep her laughing.

The moment they stepped onto the small dance floor, where three other couples were hugged up, dancing to Marvin Gaye's "Sexual Healing," the song changed. The band expertly transitioned into "Jam Tonight," an oldie by Freddie Jackson. The lead vocalist sounded so much like the legendary R&B singer that if Dexter hadn't been looking at the guy, he would've thought it was Jackson on stage.

"Whatchu know about boppin'?" Dexter asked, close to Mona's ear, referring to the old-school dance he used to do back in the day. He didn't give her a chance to respond as he held her right hand and lifted her arm over her head and spun her. He smoothly shuffled his feet and rocked his body to the beat as he guided her while still holding her hand. He smiled when she fell easily into step. She was already sexy, but dancing with her, and watching how well she grooved on the dance floor with such ease and grace, was a serious turn on.

"All right now, Ms. Mona Lisa." He grinned and spun her and she laughed. Bringing her dancing had been a good idea if that smile on her face was any indication. Activities like dancing was something he and Lillie had enjoyed while married. When he had agreed with his sponsor that it was better to refrain from dating during the early years of his recovery, he often wondered if he would get this part of his life back. It was a long time before he felt comfortable enough to go to a club for fear of relapsing.

The music slowed and Dexter pulled Mona close, his arm going easily around her small waist. "You're a great dancer," he said, as their bodies swayed to the instrumental tunes of the band.

"You're not so bad yourself." She wrapped her arms around his neck and laid her head on his chest. She fit perfectly in his arms and he held her tighter, loving how she molded against him. All evening their connection seemed to grow stronger, and being with her was something Dexter could definitely get used to.

He inhaled deeply, and the smell of gardenias filled his nostrils, only making him want to bury his face against her scented neck. He didn't know the name of the perfume she was wearing, but it was as if it had been made specifically for her. He liked everything about the woman, and the desire swirling inside of him at her closeness had him placing a gentle kiss against her head.

They were so attuned to one another, it was easy to forget they weren't the only ones in the building. This was what Dexter missed. A nice evening out with a beautiful woman, sharing in an activity they both enjoyed. Sometimes the simplest pleasures were the most fulfilling.

Hopefully, she'd agree to go out with him again.

Chapter Six

After being dropped off by an Uber driver, Dexter walked Mona to her door. They stood in the hallway, staring at each other. She hadn't been on a date in so long, she wasn't sure of the protocol for ending the night. Clearly, he wasn't sure either.

While Mona lingered in front of her door fiddling with her keys, Dexter shuffled from one foot to the other as if he was nervous, his hands shoved into his front pants pockets. He hadn't seemed anxious. Until now.

"Thank you for spending your evening with me," he finally said, the deepness of his voice sending tingles through her body. She didn't think she'd ever get used to the rumble of his baritone. The sexiness was only enhanced when he spoke quietly, like now.

"I had a wonderful time."

"I'm glad. Hopefully you'll allow me to take you out again soon."

"That would be nice. It's been a long time since I've had this much fun, and I appreciate you introducing me to new things."

"Things? Like what?"

"Like how to properly eat a slice of thin-crust pizza." She laughed and he joined in. "And I haven't gone dancing in years. I forgot how much fun it could be."

"I'm glad you had a good time. I'll let you get inside."

He stepped forward and placed a chaste kiss against her cheek, but didn't pull all the way back. Their faces were close enough for Mona to feel a whisper of his breath against her heated skin. She couldn't remember the last time her body felt so alive. Everything within her wanted to throw caution to the wind and initiate their first *real* kiss, since it didn't seem he would do it. But she couldn't. She had always carried herself as a lady, and attacking this man's mouth would definitely not be ladylike.

His gaze fell to her lips and the prolong anticipation of his next move was almost unbearable. What was he thinking? Did he not see that she wanted this as much as he did?

"May I kiss you?" he finally asked, and excitement flooded her body.

Always the gentleman.

Mona nodded and tried to relax, but the butterflies fluttering around in her gut made her feel as if she was a virgin in high school preparing for her first kiss.

Dexter eased his hand to her waist and wrapped his arm around her, bringing her flush against his incredible body. He lowered his head and Mona tilted hers slightly as they stared into each other's eyes. Moving at the same time, their lips met.

Sweet.

Gentle.

Goosebumps rose on her arms when his tongue found hers and the butterflies from moments ago went crazy. Her mind shut down. Leave it to Dexter to stoke a gently growing flame and awaken the passion that had been buried deep down inside. The feel of his body against hers reminded her of how long it had been since she'd been held so tenderly.

Mona's purse and keys slipped from her grasp and tumbled to the floor. She gave herself freely to the hunger of his kiss, matching each stroke of his tongue.

Her hands moved up his torso, loving the way his muscles bunched beneath her fingers. Just as she had imagined, he was solid. Fit for a man his age. He felt so good as he made love to her mouth, making her wonder how he'd be in bed.

One of Dexter's arms tightened around her while his other hand went to the nape of her neck when their kiss grew more urgent and exploratory. Shocked by her own eager response, Mona held on like a love-starved woman, never wanting the connection to end.

Nearby footsteps sounded and were getting closer, and Mona jerked away. She swallowed hard, her fingers going immediately to her warm lips.

Whew!

She blew out a breath and gathered herself while Dexter bent down and picked up her forgotten purse and keys. He handed her the bag as the footsteps stopped a few doors down, and they greeted her neighbor. After the guy disappeared inside his unit, Dexter spoke.

"It's late. I better let you get inside." He used the keys he hadn't returned to her and unlocked the door, before handing her the key ring. "Have a good night."

"Thank you. You too."

He stood in the hallway until Mona closed the door.

Once inside, she leaned against the door and released a contented sigh. Her mouth curved into an unconscious smile.

"I take it you had a good time?" Johnette asked as she strolled into the small foyer. Wearing an oversized T-shirt and a pair of leggings with thick socks, she looked right at home. "Well, how was it? What did you guys do? Where'd you go? Details, woman. I need details."

Mona laughed. She remembered the times when they were growing up, and she'd be the one asking a ton of questions about Johnette's dates. Her sister had been a social butterfly, rarely spending the weekends at home. Back then, Mona lived vicariously through her, wanting to know everything there was to know about boys.

She pushed away from the door. "Well, Ms. Nosey, if you must know…" Her voice trailed off when she moved farther into the house, stopping before reaching the living room that was connected to the dining room. "What in the world?"

"Oh, did I forget to mention there was a delivery while you were out."

There were vases of flowers everywhere, and not just any flowers, but irises. Her favorite.

Mona roamed around the room, inhaling the potent scent of one of the bouquets when she bent slightly to smell it. She didn't have to ask who the flowers were from. This gesture had Russell written all over it.

"Here," her sister said after plucking the small envelope from one of the bouquets.

Mona pulled out the card.

I'll die without you in my life. I can't let you go.

She read the note once more before balling it up and dropping it in a nearby trash can.

"See, that's the shit that makes me think he really is crazy. Who says stuff like that? And how did he know where you lived?" Johnette asked, her hands on her hips.

Mona glanced around the room. Flower vases covered every flat surface and…

"Wait. How'd you…you read my card?"

"Of course, I read it. I needed to know who sent this stuff, especially this time of night. Oh, and there's something else." She pointed to the breakfast bar where a square-shaped velvet box sat.

Mona strolled across the room. There really wasn't a need to look inside the box. No doubt there would be some elaborate necklace and earrings laced with diamonds. Whatever it was, she'd donate it to a charity. The last thing she needed was more jewelry, and she'd have the flowers delivered to a nearby nursing home.

She lifted the lid of the velvet box and sure enough, there was a diamond and ruby necklace with matching earrings set in white gold.

"Back to my question. If you're trying to move on, why would you tell Russell where you live?"

"I didn't. He's wealthy. When you have money, you can get anything, including my contact information."

And it was only a matter of time before he showed up.

"Anyway, enough about the loser." Johnette sat on the sofa, tucking her feet underneath her. "How was your date?"

That brought a smile to Mona's face. "It was wonderful. Let me change out of these clothes and I'll be right back."

A short while later, wearing her favorite satin lounging pajamas, Mona poured herself a glass of water. When she entered the living room, she sat on the opposite end of the sofa.

She told Johnette about her and Dexter's walk through the neighborhood and how they ended up at a romantic restaurant before they went dancing. They both had a good laugh at how Dexter showed her the proper way to eat thin-crust pizza.

"I can't ever remember having as much fun as I had tonight…ever."

"Well, it's about time you enjoyed yourself. God knows you deserve it after wasting all of those years with Russell the jerk."

Mona shook her head, hoping her sister wasn't revving up for one of her rants about how much she hated Russell.

"Dexter is a recovering alcoholic," Mona blurted.

"Whoa! Really?"

She nodded and told her about the conversation.

"Does that mean you're not going out with him again?"

"I'm not sure. He's really charming, but…"

Mona fiddled with the water glass, tracing her finger down the side and catching the condensation. While changing clothes, she'd thought about whether or not she'd go out with him again. Dating him might be asking for trouble.

"I'm not sure if I can be with an alcoholic. Even though he's been clean for five years, what if he relapses?"

"That's a tough one, sis. There are people recovering from various addictions that go on to live productive lives. Maybe get to know him and see how it goes."

"That's true."

Dexter sounded so proud when he told her how long he'd been sober. It was hard for Mona to stop eating too many cookies in one sitting. She couldn't imagine what it was like for an alcoholic to abstain from drinking.

"And I'd hate for you to miss out before even giving him a chance."

"He was adamant about never touching a drink again, but there's always a possibility. And I don't know if that's something I could deal with...if I was interested in pursuing a relationship with him. Oh, and I forgot to mention. He's looking for a wife."

The moment the words were out of her mouth, memories of the kiss they shared in the hallway filled her mind. Lips so soft and gentle, he definitely knew how to kiss. She'd be lying if she said he hadn't left an impression.

"I can't imagine Nick or Sumeera encouraging you to go out with Dexter if they thought he wasn't on the up-and-up. Besides, you never know when love is going to come a-knocking."

"We had one date. I'm keeping my options open, and remember...I'm not looking for a husband. Right now, I just want a...friend."

"I know. You keep telling me that, but what if Mr. Right comes along? Would you reconsider?" Mona opened her mouth to speak, but Johnette lifted her hand. "And if you say that Russell was your Mr. Right, I'm going to throw this pillow at you."

Mona laughed, knowing that she would do it.

"I know Russell wasn't my Mr. Right. Though he and I had some good times, I…he…he didn't make my heart skip a beat whenever he walked into a room. I didn't dream about him or run to the door excited to see him or kiss him after he'd been gone the whole day."

Johnette shook her head. "Yet, another example for why I can't wrap my brain around how or why you stayed so long. You walked in this man's shadow for years, yet—"

"Let's not start this conversation again. That was my past, and I'm trying really hard to move on and not look back. But you and Sumeera keep bringing Russell's name into every conversation."

"You're right. I won't bring up that chump's name ever again. Now, getting back to my question. If Mr. Right ever came along, would you consider marriage?"

Mona's thoughts immediately went to her date with Dexter. There was a warmth, and gentleness about him that she had never experienced. From what she could tell so far, he was definitely husband material, but she didn't need a husband.

"When Russell and I first got together, I wanted to get married and have a few children. Now, I don't want to be tied down again."

"I hear you. Let me just say, as a person who did the bachelorette thing for years, it's not all it's cracked up to be. Be smart and be safe. And while you're out here finding yourself, don't overthink everything. Have fun and take chances. I know you. You say one thing, but what you've describe is not really who you are."

Mona shook her head. "You guys think you know me."

"I'm your sister. I *do* know you."

"You also thought I was broke. Thought I had been living under Russell's thumb without looking out for my best interest. You also thought I couldn't do anything for myself. Thought I couldn't even iron a shirt."

"Okay, you're right. I thought you had gotten with the man who should remain nameless, and lost your damn mind.

I'm sorry. I'm glad you weren't as bad off as I originally thought. However, I know you well enough to know you're the marrying type despite what you say. And you might be enjoying this newfound independence, but let me tell you— being alone gets old real fast."

Mona would never admit it, but she'd had her bouts of loneliness over the last few months, which was why she had joined a dating site for *seasoned* people.

"I won't be lonely for long. I met a guy."

Johnette's brows drew together. "Besides Dexter?"

Mona nodded, a smile spreading slowly across her mouth. "I met him online last week. We're meeting for coffee tomorrow."

"Wait. Are you sure that's a good idea? It might not be safe."

"We're meeting in a public place. I'll be fine. I know a few people who have had success with online dating and they gave me some pointers."

Johnette studied her for a long moment before speaking. "Well, dang. Maybe you are ready to date. In that case, I think the speech I gave you years ago is in order. In short, remember, no glove—"

"No love. I know, I know. Though I don't think I'll need condoms anytime soon, I did purchase some when I was at the drug store last week." She giggled like a school girl when Johnette's mouth fell open. It wasn't often her sister was caught speechless.

Excitement sparked inside of Mona. She couldn't believe she was thinking about condoms at her age, but one could never be too careful.

Chapter Seven

Dexter turned on the main water valve located in the basement of his daughter and son-in-law's home. He had shut it off over an hour ago before adding hot and cold water shut-off valves under the kitchen sink. What started with him repairing a leak under the sink had turned into a bigger project.

"All right. I think that's it," he said to himself, and glanced around the floor area near the laundry room to make sure he wasn't leaving anything behind. Pulling on the chain connected to the single light bulb hanging from the ceiling, he clicked off the light and headed to the stairs.

While leaving the unfinished part of the basement, Dexter glanced around at the remodeling work that he and his son-in-law had started a month ago. Despite making good progress, everything was on hold now that they both were busy with other things. So far, they had framed in the front half of the area, converting it to a perfect family room. The installation of walls and recessed lighting, as well as staining the concrete floor, had made a huge difference. The brown leather sectional, coffee tables and a 65-inch flat-screen television rounded out the space.

Now we need to finish the rest.

Dexter climbed the stairs and pushed open the door.

"Hey, Dad. I was wondering if you were still here," Katara said when he entered the kitchen. Tall, with dark skin the color of milk chocolate, and big doe eyes, she looked so much like her mother. Especially with her hair pulled into a ponytail on top of her head. "Can I use the sink now?"

Dexter nodded. "Give it a try."

Katara turned on the water and then looked under the sink. She'd been on a conference call with a client for most of his visit. As a virtual assistant, the ability to work from home came in handy since their youngest child, who was currently napping, wasn't old enough to attend school.

Times had changed since Dexter was her age. Having a career that offered flexibility and the choice to work from home hadn't been an option when he and Lillie were raising their children.

Katara closed the cabinet door and then turned off the water. "Dad, I don't know what we would do without you." She planted a noisy kiss against his cheek.

"Hopefully, you never have to find out." Dexter placed his pipe wrench inside his toolbox.

"You've been so busy lately, I almost called J&S to send someone out," she said of Jenkins & Sons Construction.

"Well, now you can save those few dollars. Oh, that reminds me. I won't have time to hang the chandelier this afternoon. I can either stop by this weekend or early next week."

"There's no hurry. Next week is fine. Do you have time for a late lunch? I made chicken salad this morning. How about a sandwich?"

Dexter glanced at his watch. "No can do, kiddo. We're having new light fixtures installed in some of the hallways at the condominium. I'll need to leave in time to meet Jerry there at two-thirty."

Jerry Jenkins, one of Steven's grandsons and an electrician for the family's construction company, had been doing work at the condo off and on for the past couple of weeks. As the caretaker of the condo, Dexter was glad to be well connected with the best construction company in the city.

Steven had started the business some fifty years ago and when he'd been ready to retire, his grandkids decided to run the company. Most of them, including the girls, were tradesmen. Over the last ten years, they'd turned the family business into a multimillion-dollar corporation.

"Well, you have to eat," Katara said. "I'll fix you a sandwich to take with you."

"Sounds like a plan."

Dexter leaned on the back of one of the kitchen chairs, watching as his daughter moved around the open space. She chatted while she worked, telling him about his granddaughter's upcoming recital.

He appreciated her keeping him in the loop. There had been a time when he'd been estranged from his children and their families, wanting to get himself together before rejoining their lives. Despite him trying to stay clear of them, his daughter called him periodically to check in. A few years ago, after finding out how long he'd been sober and knowing he'd been struggling to find steady work, she invited him to move in with them. Shortly after that, his life started turning around.

"Have you been out with Mona again?" Katara asked, pulling a couple of sandwich bags from the drawer next to the pantry. She placed the sandwich in one and a handful of green grapes in the other.

"No. I've asked her out twice and each time she claimed to have other plans. I even saw her leaving one night...with a guy about my age. I think she was on a date."

Dexter tried convincing himself that wasn't the case, but if the way she'd been dressed was any indication, it had definitely been a date.

"Maybe I shouldn't have told her I was an alcoholic."

He had been thinking about that for the last few days. He cautioned himself to move slow, but it wasn't often someone came along and made you feel things you hadn't felt in years. While on their date, his steps were lighter. It was as if he was a new man, seeing the world through a different pair of glasses. They clicked.

After a slight hesitation, Katara spoke. "I think it's good you told her, especially if you really like this woman. *But* I'm not sure it was a good idea to tell her about your alcoholism on the first date."

"Well, I'm too old to be playing games. I think she might be *the one*. I wanted all my cards on the table."

"Wait. What? Didn't you say that was you guy's first date? How could she be *the one*? Dad, you don't even know the woman."

"I know." Dexter pushed away from the chair and strolled over to the window that overlooked a portion of the backyard. "I can't explain it. I just know that I felt more alive with her than I have in years. There's something special about her. By the end of the night, it was as if we'd known each other for years. We talked, laughed, danced, and overall had a great time together. I know it sounds crazy, but she's the one. The vibe we shared that night was the same feeling I had when I first met your mother."

"Yeah, but, um, look how that turned out," his daughter said lightly with a smile.

Dexter chuckled. There was a time he couldn't laugh about losing the woman he thought he'd be with until his death. "You know what I mean. That same…electrifying pull, for lack of a better word. Spending time with Mona only magnified that sense of…rightness." He didn't bother telling her the kiss they shared had sealed the deal for him.

"Mona, huh?"

"Yes, her name is Mona Lisa Gregory."

"Mona Lisa. Like the painting?" She giggled. "And I thought my parents were evil when giving me my name."

"Hey! You have a beautiful name."

"Yeah, a name people butcher on a daily basis. But anyway, though I don't believe in love at first sight, if you think she's special, don't give up. I say give it a few days and then call Mona *Lisa* to just talk. That way you can get a feel for what she's thinking and whether or not she might be interested in going out with you again."

"A few days? That's ridiculous. Neither of us is getting any younger. No. I'm calling her tonight. I'll see if she'd like to go out with me again. Or better yet, maybe I'll stop by her place. Then it'll be harder for her to come up with any excuses."

Katara shook her head, not looking convinced. "Fine, Dad, but if you scare her off, don't say I didn't warn you."

*

Mona shut off the timer on the stove and grabbed the oven mitts to pull the two cookie sheets out of the oven. The smell of cinnamon consumed the small kitchen, and a smile tugged at her lips. It had been a long time since she'd baked. Not since Sumeera was little and they made cinnamon-roll sugar cookies for her class, bake sales, and for Christmas gifts.

Mona's heart swelled with love at the memory. She set the trays on a baking stone for them to cool, recalling how young her daughter had been at the time. And how she'd always insist she could do everything herself, even if it meant flour and sugar ended up covering the countertops and floor. Despite the mess, they had a good time creating masterpieces in the kitchen.

She ached for those early years. The time before Russell's business took off, and when life was nice and simple.

Like it is now. Like it will stay.

Mona almost didn't recognize her current life. Days filled with yoga classes, early morning coffee on her balcony, occasional dates, and grandma day with her grandbaby was what she looked forward to now. She didn't miss the traveling, elegant events, or the dinner parties Russell needed her to host to woo clients.

Nope, her life was nice, simple and…perfect.

She glanced at the clock, surprised it was almost six. "I need to get these boxed up."

She started packing up the six-dozen oatmeal, chocolate chip, and sugar cookies that had cooled and placed them in the decorative reusable containers. She'd been baking all afternoon, since she and her neighbor were donating baked goods to a nearby homeless shelter. Giving to others in need had always been important to Mona, even though there had been a time when she would've had her cook do the baking for her. Doing the work herself was much more rewarding.

The moment she added the last container to the large shopping bag, someone knocked on her door.

"Right on time," she murmured, wiping her hands on one of the dishtowels before hurrying out of the kitchen.

She looked through the peephole and then swung the door open.

"Hey, Kelli. Come on in. I just finished packing everything up."

Kelli walked in with her micro-braids piled on top of her head and clothes that were two sizes too big. Eccentric in her own way, her style was a cross between artsy with her long multi-color skirt, and tomboyish with the white T-shirt and oversized button-up flannel shirt. Kelli had been one of the first people to befriend Mona when she moved into the complex.

"Come on into the kitchen," Mona said, leading the way.

"You are truly a godsend. I don't know what I was thinking volunteering to make twelve dozen homemade cookies." Kelli inhaled deeply and slowly released the breath. "Man, it smells amazing in here. Better than my place. The scents in here remind me of my grandma's house during the holidays. The hints of vanilla, cinnamon, and chocolate competing for attention."

Mona laughed. "I haven't baked in so long, I forgot how good it makes the house smell."

They chatted while she wrapped up a few of the extra cinnamon-roll cookies for Kelli to take with her. The rest would go to Sumeera and Nick.

"All right, I'd better get going." Kelli carried the two shopping bags to the door. "Thanks again for your help. There's no way I could've gotten all of this done today without you."

"It was my pleasure. I'll be happy to do it again sometime."

"Okay, I'm going to hold you to that. Be ready."

Mona chuckled. "I'll be ready."

Still laughing, she swung open the door and froze.

"Dexter," she gasped.

He stood on the other side of the threshold, his broad shoulders filling the doorway. As usual whenever in his presence, her body heated with the way he looked at her. Probably because it was sex-starved. How else could she explain her body's reaction? The strong response toward him wasn't normal and it was confusing.

Dexter wasn't classically handsome like Russell, who always received second glances from women in passing. Yet, whenever Mona was in Dexter's presence, giddiness soared through her like a rocket shooting through the atmosphere. What was it about this man that had her feeling bubbly inside?

Her gaze took him in. His hair had been recently cut and the clean scent of his aftershave surrounded her. He looked great in the beige Henley that stretched across his wide chest, and he had paired it with black jeans. When Mona's attention went to his eyes, that spark of desire she'd spotted when they had dinner was still there.

Neither of them said a word as his appreciative gaze did a slow glide down her body and stopped at her thick frumpy socks before returning to her face. She hadn't planned to leave the house. She'd put on the first thing her hands touched—a long-sleeved T-shirt and yoga pants. Something she wouldn't normally wear when living with Russell, not knowing when he'd bring a business associate home.

Tugging on the sleeve of her T-shirt, she fidgeted under Dexter's perusal. It was easy to get lost in his kind eyes. But when his tongue eased out of his mouth and swiped across his bottom lip, heat rush through her body. Her nipples pebbled into hard peaks behind the thin shirt at the gesture, and her whole body throbbed with need.

Goodness gracious.

Her heart raced a little faster. It didn't matter how many dates she went on, none of the men made her senses leap to life with just a look. Each time they passed in the hallway, her body tingled. There was something about the way he looked at her, his voice, and that smile that aroused her, making her feel more alive than she'd ever felt.

A throat cleared and Mona's cheeks flushed when she remembered they weren't alone. She glanced over her shoulder at Kelli, who had a knowing smirk on her face.

"Um, I guess that's my cue to get lost. Thanks again, Mona. I'll talk to you tomorrow. *And bye, Dexter,*" she said in a singsong voice as she scooted past him and hurried away, her laughter trailing behind her.

Mona touched her forehead and shook her head in embarrassment. Dexter stood off to the side, but still hadn't spoken.

"Hi," she finally said, self-consciously patting her hair, knowing she must look a wreck.

"Hi yourself. May I come in?"

God, that voice.

She gripped the doorknob tighter. "Of course. Sorry. Please come in."

When he stepped in and headed to the living room, Mona took a quick peek in the mirror hanging in the foyer and groaned. She looked worse than she thought and realized she'd gone to the door without makeup. Something she never did.

She blew out a nervous breath and adjusted her clothing. There was nothing she could do about it now. Apparently, she didn't look that bad if his earlier reaction was any indication. Then again, maybe he'd been in shock to see her without makeup.

If that was the case, that's what he got for showing up without calling.

*

"Would you like to go to the movies?" Dexter blurted the moment she entered the living room. The conversation with his daughter about his forwardness possibly scaring Mona away played in his mind and amped up his eagerness. He didn't want to make her uncomfortable, but he didn't want to let her get away, either.

"Um…"

"I'm sorry. I know I should've called first, but I haven't been able to stop thinking about you. The quick hellos in passing these last few weeks haven't been enough," he rushed to say, his heart pounding hard in his chest. "I like you, Mona, and I want to spend more time with you. Every—"

"Dexter." Mona held her hands out in front of her. "Slow down."

He stopped, took a breath and chuckled. It was like being back in high school trying to get the head cheerleader to go to the homecoming dance with him.

He ran his hand over his head and down the back of his neck and laughed at himself.

"I'm sorry. You have me all worked up looking…" He waved his hand up and down at her relaxed look, unable to find the words to describe how attractive she was. He couldn't ever remember seeing her without makeup. Personally, he liked her better without it, especially since she didn't need it. And she wasn't all dressed up. There were days she looked untouchable with her fancy clothes. He liked this look much better.

Mona frowned, her hands on her hips. "Looking like what?"

"Looking…looking sexy as hell. You're always dolled up, but this…" He did the hand thing again. "I can't think straight when you're so tempting and…sexy."

Still frowning, Mona dropped her arms to her sides and glanced down at her attire. She returned her attention to him.

"You have to be kidding. This," she pointed at herself, "is what has you acting weird?"

Dexter laughed harder. "This visit is not going the way I planned."

After work he'd intended to cook dinner and sit back and watch basketball. Instead, he showered, scarfed down a salad, and before he could stop himself, he was standing at her door.

"Back to my original question. Would you like to go and see the latest Morgan Freeman movie with me?"

She snapped her finger. "That's who you remind me of. I've been puzzling my brain since the first time you spoke to me trying to figure out who you sound like. That deep, sensual baritone is just like Morgan Freeman's."

A slow smile spread across Dexter's lips. "Sensual, huh?" Over the years, people had often commented on the deepness and the power behind his voice. But hearing Mona call his voice sensual had him sticking his chest out, feeling as if he could conquer the world.

Mona opened her mouth, but nothing came out and she shut it. That shyness he'd witnessed more often than not was back and so was her adorable smile.

Deciding not to pick on her, he asked, "So, how about a movie?"

"When?"

"Right now."

"*Now?*"

"The movie starts in thirty minutes."

She glanced down at her outfit again. "I would love to go, but that doesn't give me enough time to shower and ch—"

"You look amazing, Mona. All you need to do is slip into a pair of shoes and grab a jacket."

She twisted her bottom lip between her teeth as if seriously considering his invite.

"I'll give you three minutes," he prompted.

"Make it five and we have a deal."

She didn't wait for a response. Instead, she rushed to the back of the condo. Exactly five minutes later she returned. She had pulled her hair into a ponytail at the nape of her neck, added gloss to her lips, slipped into a pair of knee-high boots, and wore a short leather jacket.

Dexter grinned, impressed at the speed in which it took her to look even sexier. "You look great."

She laughed. "We really need to get your eyes checked."

He liked this side of her. Relaxed and carefree.

When she started to move past him, Dexter reached out and grabbed her hand. Without thinking, he pulled her to him and captured her mouth with his. She gasped, but that didn't stop him from taking what he wanted. She kissed him back with a hunger that rivaled his, and excitement charged through his body.

He had been dreaming about kissing her again, wanting to confirm that the first time wasn't a fluke. That he hadn't imagined how perfect her body felt against his. Or how kissing her was like a fantasy come true.

As their tongues tangled, the kiss sang through his veins, sending blood rushing from his brain to the lower part of his body.

Nope, it hadn't been a fluke, he thought, as Mona's arms went around his neck, deepening their connection. The lip-lock was like a soldering heat that joined metals and Dexter never wanted to let her go.

Mona didn't know yet, but before long she'd be all his.

Chapter Eight

"Good morning, my love," Mona said in a singsong tone when she opened the door.

"Well, aren't we chipper this morning. I take it you've finally found a prince through the dating site. No more frogs?" Sumeera walked in, lugging Chanelle in her car seat, and a diaper bag and purse flung over her shoulder. "Mmm, smells like pancakes. You know you don't have to feed me every time I drop the baby off."

"I love feeding you," Mona said. She lifted a sleeping Chanelle from the car seat and cradled her in her arms. "My little cutie-pie is getting so big. She's growing too fast."

"I know. I can't believe she's four months. The best part is she's slept through the last three nights."

"That's wonderful. I bet you and Nick have enjoyed the uninterrupted sleep."

"I have, but Nick is still up every few hours checking on her."

Mona removed the baby's hat and jacket. "I'm sure he'll start sleeping through the night again soon." She and Sumeera shared a laugh.

"You look different." Sumeera shrugged out of her coat. She laid it on the white upholstered chair across from the sofa where Mona was holding Chanelle. "Having a social life must agree with you. Who's the lucky guy?"

Mona couldn't stop the smile from spreading across her face. Ever since her movie date with Dexter a few weeks ago, she hadn't been able to think of much else. The man dominated all of her free time, and she had no complaints. She had even stopped hanging out on the online dating site.

"I've been spending time with Dexter."

A smile broke free on her daughter's face. "Really? I thought you decided not to see him again. What changed?"

"I don't know. He asked me to a movie weeks ago, and since then, I've been seeing him practically every day." The last few days, their relationship had changed. Her feelings for him had grown considerably, and their intense kisses had turned into heavy petting sessions.

"I can't believe you haven't said anything."

Mona saw Sumeera several times a week, giving her plenty of opportunities to tell her about Dexter. The only excuse she could come up with for not sharing the news was that she wanted to keep her and Dexter's growing attraction between them. Besides, for months Mona claimed to not want a serious relationship, preferring a friend-with-benefits type of arrangement. Now she wasn't so sure. Some days she still wanted her freedom, then other days, she loved what was developing between her and Dexter.

"By that huge smile on your face, I take it things are going very, *very* well."

Mona grinned and nodded while standing with Chanelle, who hadn't awakened. "Go ahead and start eating. I'm going to lay her down. Then I'll tell you about me and Dexter."

Mona took Chanelle to the master bedroom where she had a traveling crib set up. Before laying her down, she kissed the baby on the top of her head. Holding her close, she soaked up her baby scent. Grandma days, when she babysat, were the best days of the week.

She laid Chanelle in the crib and made sure the baby monitor was on before leaving the room.

"Okay, tell me what's going on with you guys," Sumeera said, when Mona walked into the kitchen. She had found the pancakes, hash browns, and sausage Mona left in the warmer. "Is this getting serious?"

Mona set the mug of coffee she'd been drinking into the microwave and heated it up.

"Like I mentioned to your aunt, I'm not looking for anything serious, but I'm enjoying his company." She sounded like a broken record, but she wanted to keep reminding herself of the plan to stay unattached.

She told Sumeera about some of their dates and how she felt more comfortable with him than any other man she'd been out with. After dinner the night before, they went for ice cream at Graeter's, where conversation flowed effortlessly. Not only that, but now Mona was addicted to Graeter's treats. The popular ice cream shop had lived up to its reputation of being the best.

For weeks now, she and Dexter had fallen into a comfortable routine. Having an early breakfast and spending their evenings together eating, talking and some nights watching TV had become their norm. What Mona enjoyed most was despite how tired he might be at the end of the day, he always made time for her. She hated comparing him and Russell, but most days it was hard not to. Dexter made her feel as if they were a team, taking care of each other. With him, she felt cherished, protected, and appreciated.

"I knew Dexter was a sweetheart from the first time I met him. I'm glad you guys are getting along."

"He's like a big teddy bear. Warm and...cuddly," Mona said, her heart thumping a little faster against her ribcage as she relived their goodnight make-out session. Even in remembrance, the intimacy of the night and being wrapped in his strong arms promised of better things to come.

Sumeera stood and rinsed her dishes before placing them in the dishwasher. "Does this mean you're going to date him exclusively now?"

Mona took a tentative sip of her now-steamy coffee. Dexter was the kindest man she'd ever met and his even-tempered personality made it easy to like him. "Yes, but he understands I'm not looking for a serious commitment. Only a friend…a really, *really* good friend."

Sumeera laughed and Mona smiled behind the rim of her mug.

"I assume that's code for um…bedmate?"

"Something like that."

"Wow, I never thought I'd see the day when I'd be talking in code with my mother about sex."

Mona laughed when Sumeera gave an exaggerated shudder of mock disgust.

For the first time in her life, she wasn't shy or ashamed about discussing her sexual needs or her desire to have a sex partner. Until recently, she'd been afraid her libido had retired. But each kiss and the sensual touch of Dexter's hands on her body made her think otherwise. It was only a matter of time before they took their budding friendship to the next level.

Sumeera went into the bedroom to kiss the baby, then grabbed her coat from the living room.

"All right, I have to get out of here. I put Chanelle's bottles in the fridge, and anything else needed is in her bag." Mona walked her to the door. "As usual, breakfast was great, and I know I say you don't have to feed me each time I drop off the baby, but I'm glad you do."

"It's my pleasure, honey."

"Glad to hear that." Sumeera grinned and hugged her. Mona's heart burst with love each time she held her daughter, never wanting to release her. Every day she thanked God for this second chance to be in Sumeera's life.

"Oh, shoot," Sumeera said after they pulled apart. "I forgot to tell you. I might have found you the perfect spot for your boutique."

"Really? Where?"

"Nate and Uncle Ben purchased a property that has retail space on the first floor," Sumeera said, of Nick's twin brother and their uncle. "The place needs work, but based on the photos and the information I've received, I think it's perfect for what you're looking for. I'll let you know when we can look at it."

Excitement bubbled inside of Mona. Seemed her whole life was falling into place. She was almost finished with her business plan, and just the other day she and Dexter had discussed logistics. He was willing to handle renovations if she found a place that needed work.

Only a matter of time before my dream is a reality.

Chapter Nine

Hours later, Mona sat in the glider positioned in a corner of her bedroom, rocking Chanelle.

"You are the cutest little girl God ever created," she cooed to her grandbaby who rewarded her with a sleepy smile. Mona nuzzled her neck, eliciting a little giggle.

From week to week she marveled at the baby's milestones. Lately, she had to dodge Chanelle's tiny hands. Her little one was at the stage where she was grabbing at anything in reach, including Mona's hoop earrings and her hair.

"I don't know why you're fighting sleep. Close those big pretty eyes. When you get my age, you're going to wish you had time to take naps."

When Chanelle's eyes started drooping, Mona hummed a lullaby she used to sing to Sumeera.

"How could I have stayed away from your mommy so long?" she said to a now-sleeping Chanelle, brushing the back of her fingers down the baby's chubby cheek. "Never again. I'm sticking around, and if I'm lucky, I'll get more grandbabies."

Mona kissed the baby's forehead before laying her in the crib. She walked back into the living room and picked up the toys and the blanket from the floor.

She glanced at the thin watch on her wrist and her thoughts went immediately to Dexter. Normally, he called or stopped by at least once during the day, but she hadn't heard from him. She shouldn't be surprised. Each day seemed busier than the next, since he was juggling his handyman business as well as taking care of the condominium complex. She didn't know where he found the energy to do all that he did.

Mona had just placed the last of Chanelle's toys in the small container on the side of the sofa when the intercom buzzed. She hurried across the room to keep whoever was ringing her from doing it again.

"Hello."

"Mona, it's me. Let me in."

Mona's pulse jumped and she pushed away from the wall, surprised to hear Russell's voice. It had been days since she'd heard from him. She thought he had finally moved on.

When the intercom rang again, she buzzed him in. He couldn't be there. Nick and Sumeera had a restraining order, preventing him from being within five hundred feet of them, and that included Chanelle.

Mona didn't bother waiting for him to knock, she opened the door, prepared to send him away knowing he wouldn't leave her alone without saying what he had to say. Sumeera wasn't due to pick the baby up for another couple of hours, and Mona wanted him gone. No way would she let him ruin her time with Chanelle. And that's exactly what would happened if Nick ever found out about this visit. He was fiercely protective of his family, and rightfully so.

"What are you doing here?" she asked in a harsh whisper when Russell made it to the top of the landing.

"Hello to you, too, love." He leaned in to kiss her cheek, but she turned her head before he could make contact.

"You can't be here."

"You're not going to invite me in?"

"No. You have five minutes. What do you want?" She stepped into the hall and closed the door slightly, not wanting to be out of earshot of Chanelle.

"Who's in there?" Russell asked, his jaw clenched. He made a move to go around her, but she stopped him with a hand on his chest. "You have a man in there?"

"Our granddaughter. So either tell me what you want or leave."

"Not before we talk and before I finally meet my grandbaby."

Mona shook her head. "That's not going to happen and you know why."

"This is ridiculous!" he yelled. "I have a right to see her."

"You gave up that right when you manhandled our daughter."

"That was self-defense! She attacked me!"

That was true. Before deciding to relocate to Cincinnati, Mona had flown to town with Russell earlier in the year, and had stopped by Sumeera and Nick's home. What was supposed to be a nice visit, had quickly gotten out of hand when Russell tried blackmailing Sumeera. He claimed he wouldn't sign a pending, multimillion-dollar contract between his company and Jenkins & Sons Construction if she didn't agree to move back to New York and take over his property development business. Heated words were exchanged and Sumeera, who they later found out was pregnant, physically lashed out at Russell. When he tried to subdue her, Nick returned home to find Russell holding onto Sumeera's wrists, and all hell broke loose. Since then Nick and Sumeera wanted nothing to do with her father.

"Russell, you have to leave."

"Fine. Don't let me see her, but you and I need to talk. Now."

Just then her neighbor opened the door and looked out into the hallway. No doubt Russell's loud voice prompted her to investigate. The building was normally quiet. Most people worked during the day, and those on her floor who were home, were retirees or worked from home.

"Come in, but you can't stay long. Sumeera will be here soon and she can't know you were here."

Mona gave a slight wave to her neighbor and hurried Russell inside, hoping she wouldn't regret doing so.

"This has to stop," she said the moment she closed the door. "You can't keep calling, sending gifts and dropping by whenever you want."

"I can't stay away from you. You know that. I don't sleep well without you in my bed." He reached for her hand and brought her fingers to his lips, kissing the back of them. "I miss you."

She slid her hand from his and took a good look at him as they stood in the small foyer. Russell never left the house unless well-groomed and immaculately dressed. Today, however, he looked as if he had slept in his dark suit. The two-day scruff on his cheeks and chin was also out of character.

Instead of commenting on his appearance, she said, "You have to let me go, and stop calling. We've already talked about this. We don't want the same things, and I should've left sooner."

"Don't say that. You were happy being with me. We were happy together."

"Not for a long time. I've changed and so have you."

"I'm the same man you fell in love with. I'm sorry if I've been so caught up in work and my career, but I've given you everything a woman could want."

"Not everything."

He released an exasperated sigh. "Mona, I thought what we had was enough for you. We had a good thing going until you walked out."

"There's no sense in us rehashing this conversation. I've already told you more times than I can count for years now, that those things weren't enough for me. But you ignored my desires. You knew I wanted my own fashion boutique. You knew I wanted marriage and more children."

"I didn't ignore you. I just didn't understand why you wanted a store. There's not enough money to be made in that. And what was the point of marriage? We were together every day for over thirty years. All getting married would've done was added a piece of paper signed by a judge or a minister saying we were married. You've always felt like my wife."

"But I wasn't!"

"And as for kids, you didn't take care of the one we had, sending her to live with your sis—"

"Don't you dare put that on me!" she seethed, anger gripping every nerve in her body as she slowly approached him. "It was your suggestion that Sumeera stay in the States while we expanded the business overseas. You claimed as a teenager it wasn't a good idea to drag her around the world, especially when school started back. And crazy me, I listened to you! Besides, your inconsistent behavior worried me. I had to make sure my child was somewhere safe."

"Our daughter was always safe with me!"

Mona had had every intention of getting her daughter back once they returned to the States, but Sumeera preferred Cincinnati, and Mona hadn't been sure of Russell's mental state when they returned. There were times when he could be the nicest man, but on occasion, he'd be awful toward people, behaving like a different person. She tolerated him out of concern, and because…outside of being a little controlling, he had treated her well.

"Honey, I'm sorry. You're right. All of this is on me. But please let me make it up to you." He gripped her shoulders before his hands moved up to her face, cupping her cheeks.

Mona shook out of his hold. "It's too late."

"You're a part of me. I'll do whatever you want." He rubbed his forehead, seeming more agitated. "Besides…I need you more than ever. I had to fire Mavis."

"Why?"

"She was stealing from me. Every week, some of my clothes were missing. I even caught her taking some out of the closet the other day."

Mona frowned. "Are you sure she wasn't taking them to the cleaners? She has no reason to take your clothes, Russell." Mavis, their housekeeper, was in her mid-sixties, and a divorced mother of two grown daughters. Mona couldn't see the woman, who had been nothing but loyal to them for over twenty years, stealing.

"I know she was stealing them!" he snarled, running his hand over his head as he paced the small area. Tension bounced off of him in waves. "You need to stop this nonsense and come home."

Mona didn't respond. Instead she watched as his agitation from moments ago dissipated almost instantly. He smiled and folded his arms across his chest, and that confident demeanor she was used to was back.

Observing him was like watching an episode of Dr. Jekyll and Mr. Hyde.

"Is this about Henry?" he asked quietly.

"Who?"

"Henry…the doorman. I talked with him about his flirting and told him to stay away from you."

Shock hit Mona full force. "You did what?"

Henry was in his seventies and one of the nicest people she'd ever met. He was happily married, and had been for over fifty years. He never flirted.

"Listen, you don't have to worry about him bothering you anymore. I told the building manager that I thought it was time Henry retired. They're going to take care of—"

"Stop." Mona shook her head and put her hands up. "Just stop. Russell, you need help. *Professional* help."

He stood near the living room entrance, a puzzled expression on his face. It was as if he was trying to process what she was saying. Her heart ached for him, and she wasn't sure how to help him.

"Russell, how did you get here?"

"Oh." He snapped out of his trance and glanced at the Rolex on his wrist. "Darren's outside waiting for us."

"He came to Cincinnati with you?" she asked. Darren was Russell's longtime driver and friend.

"Yeah, I've been doing a lot of traveling. Instead of hiring a driver in different cities, it's easier to have Darren travel with me."

"Yeah, yeah, that's good," Mona said, more to herself than Russell. Surely Darren had noticed the changes. Maybe if she gave him the therapist's information, he could see to Russell getting the help he needed.

"Why don't you get your bags and we can head out," Russell said, and pointed his thumb over his shoulder to her living space. "I have a meeting in Chicago tomorrow afternoon, but we can go to my hotel and talk. Then fly to Chicago, have dinner at Alina's tonight, and then you can shop while I'm at my meeting tomorrow."

Mona placed her hand on her chest, trying to keep her emotions in check as her heart broke for him. She no longer loved him, but she would always care about his well-being.

"Sumeera will be here soon. You have to leave. You can't be here."

He released a low growl. "This is ridiculous. I would never hurt my own child. That man of hers has brainwashed her. I'll stay and tell her th—"

"No." Mona pulled the door open. "Please…just go. I don't want any trouble."

"I told you. I'm not leaving!"

"Yes. You. Are!"

"What's going on here?"

Mona startled at Dexter's booming baritone. He stood in the hallway, his gaze steady on her ex before turning his attention to her. He looked so tired and he was still in his work clothes.

"You okay?" He stepped in and closed the door. His arm went immediately around her waist. Normally his touch was welcomed, but not now. Russell was too volatile to witness any affection between them, and she had no idea what he was capable of right now.

"I'm fine. *Russell* was just le—"

"Who the hell are you?" Russell asked. His gazed zoomed in on Dexter's arm around her waist before looking back and forth between them. "What's going on here? I know you haven't taken up with this..." He looked Dexter up and down, turning up his arrogant nose as if smelling something bad. "This...this broke-ass bum."

Mona gasped. "Get out!" She pointed to the door, ready to physically throw him out.

"You heard the lady. Let's go." Dexter yanked the door open, his face a mask of fury.

"I don't know who you think you are, but I'm not going any-damn-where. Not without *my* woman. So *you* can show yourself out!" Russell thundered.

Dexter stepped to him and Mona grabbed hold of the back of his sweatshirt. The men were about the same height, but where Russell had a runner's build, Dexter was built like a defensive lineman. It wouldn't take much for him to pummel Russell.

"Either you leave peacefully, or I will throw your ass out. Better yet, maybe you would prefer the cops to escort you off the premises." Dexter pulled his cell phone from the front pocket of his jeans. He knew about the incident with Nick, Sumeera, and the restraining order.

Mona could hear Chanelle through the monitor. She wasn't crying, but she was slowly waking up, her cooing growing a little more frustrated. It was only a matter of time before her cries would be heard without the baby monitor.

Dexter must have heard her, too, because he glanced at Mona and nodded toward the bedrooms. But there was no way she was leaving the two of them before making sure Russell was gone.

"What's it going to be?" Dexter held up his cell phone. "Are you leaving, or do I need to call the cops?"

Standing next to Dexter, Mona watched as an evil sneer spread across Russell's face. She almost didn't recognize him.

Panic swept through her as he stepped to Dexter, getting right in his face. To Dexter's credit, he didn't budge. The fierceness on his face was as if he was daring Russell to make the wrong move.

"Sure, you can walk me out. Then I can explain to you why you'll never be man enough to handle a woman like her. She will *never* be yours. She'll *always* be mine."

"I am not yours, damn it!" Mona snapped, jabbing him in the arm with her finger. "We are done! And if you ever come here again, I'm calling the cops myself. Now go!"

"Mona."

"Goodbye, Russell."

Chanelle started crying and Mona glanced at Dexter. The warmth she usually saw in his eyes when he looked at her wasn't there. Surely, he wasn't believing the crap her ex was spewing. He was everything Russell wasn't and she had to make sure he knew that.

"Go ahead and take care of the baby. I'll show this guy out and be right back," he said.

She nodded and headed for the bedroom.

"This isn't over, Mona!" Russell yelled.

Mona didn't bother turning back. She planned to call Darren and pass on the therapist's number. After that, she was done. Even if it meant changing her phone number and getting some type of security. They were officially over and it was past time she made herself clear.

Chapter Ten

Dexter's stomach seethed with trepidation as he paced his living room floor. Moving around did nothing to slow the adrenaline pumping through his veins as he listened to his AA sponsor, Warren, on the other end of the phone. Warren had seen him through some tough times over the years, and Dexter wouldn't have reached the five-year mark of his sobriety without him.

But right now, the overwhelming urge to have a drink could ruin everything he had worked so hard for.

"Was the conversation with this Russell guy the only thing that set you off today?"

Dexter slowly released the pent-up breath that had been lodged in his chest for the last few minutes. When he escorted Mona's ex to the door, he wanted to punch the asshole for bothering her. What should've been an easy task of kicking him out and then locking the door behind him had turned into a ten-minute verbal match, mainly on Russell's part. Dexter had never been a man who worried about what others said about him, but for some reason, the man's assessment of him cut deeply.

"Honestly, the urge has been building all day despite my morning starting out pretty good. I had coffee with Mona, but the day went downhill from there. I don't mind hard work, but between an apartment flooding, and then going across town to strip hardwood floors for one of my customers, I'm mentally and physically tired. So when I heard arguing coming from Mona's unit, my attitude took a nose dive."

She was probably wondering why he hadn't returned after escorting Russell out. Truth was, he had been in no condition to face her. He needed to get his craving under control before he saw her again.

"When you called, you said you wanted to strangle the guy. I've never known you to be violent, Dex. I'm hoping you weren't serious."

Dexter huffed out a frustrated breath. "No...as long he stays away from here and away from Mona." He knew he shouldn't be threatening anyone, but he couldn't help the fierce desire to protect her. Part of him really did feel like strangling the pompous ass. "He said some things..."

"Some things like what?"

"That I wasn't good enough for her. That I would never be able to please her or keep a woman like her." Those comments probably wouldn't have affected him had he not thought them a time or two himself. Mona was a special woman and the more time he spent with her, the deeper he was falling for her. She carried herself like a woman of privilege, but never made him feel like a second-class citizen. Never made him feel like a man who had more baggage than he knew what to do with, and not like a man who was an alcoholic.

Dexter dropped down in his recliner and rubbed his forehead.

"I don't think I can do this, Warren."

"Do what, Dex?"

"Keep seeing Mona." His friend, Sean, had been right. She was way out of his league and he had been kidding himself thinking otherwise. "She deserves someone who doesn't have baggage. I wish you could meet her. She's classy, smart, gorgeous, and she's all I think about. When I'm with her, everything feels right except…"

When Dexter didn't continue, Warren spoke. "She doesn't know about the accident. You know you have to tell her."

"I know, and I will. I want her in my life forever, Warren, but I don't know if I can—"

"You're not the same man you were years ago. You've come a long way and have rebuilt your life. You have a good handyman business, and now you're the caretaker of the condominium. Don't let this guy's comments shake your confidence. Remember, he's a man who lost the woman you're with. Of course, he's going to say anything he can to make you look bad in her eyes, and to make you doubt yourself."

"Well, it worked."

"What did Mona say?"

"Most of what he said was outside, but before Russell left her place, she told him that she wasn't his. It wasn't until we stepped outside that he really started talking trash. Had it not been for his driver stepping between us, I'd probably be in jail for whooping his ass."

"I'm glad it didn't come to that."

Yeah, me too.

Dexter never wanted to see the inside of a jail cell again.

That last thought was like a stab to the chest, reminding him of the conversation he still needed to have with Mona. Each day they spent together, he considered telling her about his past, but it never seemed to be the right time.

"Dex, do you want me to meet you at an AA meeting? I could be at the one near you in about fifteen min—"

"No. No, I'm good, Warren. Talking to you is helping. I think part of my problem tonight is that my conscience is weighing on me."

"About the guy?"

Dexter stood at the living room window and looked out over the darkened parking lot. "It's Mona. She's…she's my heart, man. Every minute we spend together, my feelings for her grow deeper and deeper, but I'm way out of my element here."

"How so?"

Prior to dating Mona, Dexter knew he was ready to find the perfect woman and settle down. He had hoped to connect with someone like Lillie, but that's not what he found. Both women were kind and generous. Yet, that's where the personality similarities stopped. Lillie was a homemaker, and her whole world centered around the children and him for a while, whereas Mona loved her child in her own way, but she wanted more than motherhood.

Dexter had no doubt that if Russell hadn't belittled her ideas, she would've owned a couple of businesses by now. She was like a baby bird that never had a chance to spread her wings. She also seemed willing to try anything once. He had invited her to go hiking with him tomorrow, and she agreed. Their dates had included everything from skating to laser tag, and he had even taught her how to change out a faucet.

When he was married, there was nothing he could've done to talk Lillie into doing anything as daring as laser tag. While Mona came across as shy, a better description of her would be reserved…with a hidden adventurous side.

"Dexter?" Warren called out, snapping Dexter out of his thoughts and back to their conversation.

"Mona and I haven't known each other long, but… I can't really explain it. That powerful connection I experienced when we first met is stronger than ever. At first, I thought maybe it was infatuation, but it's more than that."

"And these feelings are a bad thing?"

"They are when she doesn't know my whole story. They are when my conscience is eating away at me. I just don't know if she'll hold my past sins against me."

"Dex, you haven't had a drink in years. You've changed."

"I know and you know, but will she see that? Or will she see me as another problem man she's getting stuck with?" Dexter rubbed the back of his neck, trying to work out some of the tension. "Either way, I need to be totally straight with her because…"

After a long pause, Warren said, "Because you're in love with her."

Dexter wasn't sure it was love, especially since they'd only known each other for a short time. Yet, she was all he thought about from the moment he opened his eyes each morning until he fell asleep at night. He wanted to be with her all the time, and each day he came face to face with her, it was as if the dark clouds of his past were replaced with sunshine. He loved the way she made him feel. Complete. Whole. Needed. Wanted.

I'm in love with her, he admitted to himself.

By the time Dexter and Warren finished their call, Dexter was glad he had contacted his sponsor. Sometimes all it took was speaking his fears out loud. He might not be able to give Mona everything she'd been accustomed to, but he had the means to offer her a nice comfortable life. Each day they grew closer, but he wasn't sure her feelings for him were as strong as his were for her. But no way was he letting her pretentious asshole of an ex ruin what they were building.

Dexter removed his sweatshirt as he headed to his bedroom for a shower. He had changed his mind. Going to an AA meeting wouldn't hurt right now, especially knowing he had to come clean with Mona.

"I have to tell her," he mumbled when he stepped into the bathroom. "I have to tell her everything."

Let's just hope she doesn't kick me to the curb.

*

Mona changed into a short-sleeved red wrap dress that stopped above her knees, hoping that seeing her in the outfit would make Dexter feel better. She smoothed her hands over her hips, loving how soft the garment felt against her skin.

"Maybe this little number will give him some energy," Mona murmured. Eagerness swelled inside of her as she slipped into a pair of two-inch heels the same color as the dress. When she'd first considered dating at her age, the idea scared her to death. But who knew it could be this exciting? She hadn't had this much fun in years.

Hurrying to the bathroom, she washed her hands, then headed to the kitchen to pack up the dinner she'd made for her and Dexter.

He hadn't called or returned after escorting Russell out. Even after several calls to him, she hadn't been able to reach him until after Sumeera picked up Chanelle. Mona heard the weariness in his voice as Dexter told her it had been a long day and that he planned to go to bed early. But the promise to see her tomorrow for their hiking adventure wasn't enough. She wanted to be with him tonight.

He looked so tired when she'd seen him earlier, but Mona suspected something else was going on. After spending every evening together for weeks, tired or not, he never cancelled on her. No doubt Russell had caused trouble outside.

Once Mona had everything she needed, she headed downstairs. Standing in front of Dexter's door, she started second-guessing her decision to show up without informing him.

No turning back now.

She knocked a couple of times before the door swung open. Dexter stood before her in a white T-shirt and gray jogging pants and white socks on his feet. With the small distance between them, his shower-fresh scent snagged her attention and saturated every one of her senses.

"Hi," she finally said.

"You're...gorgeous. What's the occasion?" He glanced at the picnic basket she held at her side.

"I made dinner and I didn't want to eat alone."

"Ah, sweetheart." His large hand cupped her cheek. "I'm sorry I abandoned you tonight. I only..." He ran his hand over his mouth and blew out a breath. "I'm sorry. Come in."

Dexter grabbed the basket from her and closed the door with his foot. Before she could walk past him, he pulled her against his body.

Mona's pulse amped up with his nearness and her hands fisted the front of his T-shirt at the fiery desire radiating in his dark eyes. She had waited all day to be wrapped in his embrace.

"I failed to greet you properly when I saw you earlier." He nipped at her top lip and then her bottom one before claiming her mouth completely. It amazed her how, with little effort, he could get her body revved up and begging for more.

When the kiss turned more heated, Mona melted against him. The caress of his lips on her mouth was like…was like coming home. She would never tire of his delicious kisses or the way he held her in his arms making her feel cherished. Making her feel loved.

But each day with him challenged her self-control. Making it harder to fight the all-consuming desire running rampant through her body. She wanted him more than she had ever wanted a man in her life, and it scared her to death.

When they finally came up for air, she stared into Dexter's eyes, seeing within his orbs what she felt inside. They both wanted more. Instead of voicing that thought, she said, "That was nice…and well worth the wait."

He flashed her a grin that warmed her insides, making her glad that she decided to come to him.

Holding her hand, he ushered her to the small dining area that was connected to the newly-painted living room. She thought the bluish-gray on the walls would be too dark but had to admit it warmed up the space and went great with the brown furniture.

"Everything smells delicious," Dexter said and grabbed plates while Mona unloaded the basket. Once they set the table, they said a quick prayer and dug in.

Mona sat to the right of him as they ate, glancing at him between bites. She didn't miss the way he rubbed the back of his neck and rolled his shoulders throughout their meal. He looked exhausted, but never complained about anything, even now.

Maybe the long hours were starting to wear on him. Whatever was going on was bothering him, and Mona had a feeling it had everything to do with Russell's visit.

Normally conversation flowed effortlessly with Dexter leading the topics, but not tonight. She tried keeping the subjects neutral, not wanting to ruin the evening by discussing her ex, but apparently, she needed to say something.

"We need to talk," he said on a huff, and pushed his chair back from the table. "I need to tell—"

"Dexter." Mona set down her fork. "I'm sorry about this evening. I didn't mean for you to have to deal with Russell, and I'm so sorry about what he said to you. I had no idea he would show up. And just so you know, I haven't seen him in months and I have no intention of getting back with him. I—"

"The guy is unstable, Mona. I only spent a few minutes with him and could tell that he's a match waiting to be struck. Why would you let him in, especially with Chanelle there? Both of you could've been in danger."

"He wouldn't hurt us."

"You don't know that!" he snapped, then closed his eyes and sighed. He finally looked at her. "I'm sorry, but anything could've happened with him here."

Mona searched Dexter's worried eyes. Unease swept through her. Something else was going on. He looked as if he had the weight of the world on his shoulders.

She wiped her hands on her napkin and stood. He watched her as she moved around to the back of his chair without saying a word. She placed her hands on his shoulders and started squeezing and kneading the area before moving up to the base of his neck. Using her thumbs in a circular motion, she worked on the tension in his tight muscles, increasing the pressure when he moaned in pleasure.

"I knew Russell wouldn't leave until he had his say," she said quietly, as she continued to massage his upper body. "I hadn't planned to let him into my unit, but he got loud in the hallway. I let him in with every intention of making it clear that he and I were done. Then you showed up."

She continued working her hands in silence, hoping she was making him feel better. If the way his head fell back and his eyes closed on a moan was any indication, she was doing a good job.

Moments later, Dexter reached over his shoulder and grasped her right hand. He tugged gently and pulled her around the chair and to the front of him, placing her between his thighs. He was a big guy. Even sitting, he could almost look her in the eye.

"Thank you," he said when their gazes connected.

Dexter released her and his hands went to her hips, bringing her closer. His face was eye-level with her breasts. Mona wasn't sure what was coming next, but she ran her hands over his shoulder, up his neck, and cupped his face between her hands. The scruff on his cheeks prickled her palms.

Dexter opened his mouth to speak, but closed it and shook his head. Whatever was on his mind was really bothering him. Part of her wanted to know what was wrong, but then that other part of her...

He dropped his forehead to the valley of her breasts and released a frustrated sigh. Mona moved her hands over the top of his head. Placing a kiss against his temple, she hoped to give him some type of peace for whatever troubled him.

He lifted his head slowly, unspoken pain glowed in his eyes. "Mona...you mean so much to me." His words were filled with so much conviction, she felt them to her soul. "But there's something I need to...I need to tell you."

Mona brushed the pad of her thumb over his cheek as she searched his face. This kind, captivating, gentle man had brought more joy into her life in the past few weeks than she had experienced in years. She hated seeing him so unsettled and it was probably because of her. There was no telling what Russell had said or done on his way out the door. His words alone could cut a man deep, but Dexter could hold his own with her ex.

"How about if we save talking for later...or better yet, for the morning?" She stepped back forcing him to loosen his hold on her hips. Her hands shook a little when she reached for the knotted belt holding her wrap dress closed. Undoing the tie, she let the soft garment fall open, and then glanced at Dexter.

His gaze started at her breasts, covered in red lace and worked its way down her body until he stopped at the matching bikini panties. Her body wasn't as tight as it once was, but the spark in his eyes made her feel as if she had the curves of a twenty-year-old.

A low whistle filled the quietness of the room, and a small smile tugged up the corner of his lips. "It's a good thing I have a strong heart. Otherwise, seeing you looking this sexy would've given me a heart attack. You're stunning."

Mona laughed, suddenly feeling a little bolder with her impromptu seduction scene. She let the dress slide down her arms and puddle on the hard wood floor. Feeling empowered with the way he continued checking her out, she took a step forward, bringing her body within reach.

After a slight hesitation, he eased her closer and their lips met. So tender. So enticing. A whimper slipped through Mona as a quiver raked over her flesh. When her arms went around his neck, deepening the kiss, Dexter ravished her mouth. He kissed her with a hunger that matched her own and their moans grew louder.

As he loved on her mouth, his large hands journeyed up the side of her body. Exploring. Squeezing. Kneading her heated flesh. Her sex clenched with need at the thrilling sensation of his lips against her cheek, then her chin, and on down to her neck.

Every nerve within her was on high alert and she couldn't ever remember being this turned on.

Without a word, Dexter stood. Holding her hand, he guided her to his bedroom. Mona had been in there once.

One night when he had cooked for her, she'd worn a fancy blouse and he encouraged her to change into one of his flannel shirts so she could be more comfortable. That's when she'd had a chance to admire his huge four-poster bed that took up much of the room. She had secretly wondered if she'd ever get a chance to lay in it.

Tonight, she knew the answer.

Chapter Eleven

Once they were near the bed, Dexter's hungry gaze took her in. He felt like the biggest asshole for not telling her about the accident, but he couldn't think straight with her standing before him in the skimpy lingerie. All he wanted to do was unwrap this beautiful gift that he'd been given.

He couldn't believe she had come to him, prepared to give herself to him completely. This by far was her boldest move to date.

She was so damn pretty. Her hair hung in loose curls around her shoulders, only adding to her sexiness. The adventurous glint in her eyes matched perfectly with the lace bra and panties, and her luscious curves called to him. She definitely didn't have the body of a fifty-plus-year-old woman.

He zoned in on her full breasts and nipples pushing against the thin material, and his body tightened. Blood rushed from his brain, and shot to the lower part of his body. There was no way he'd be able to hide his growing erection wearing sweatpants, and at the moment, he wasn't trying to. He wanted her to see how much he desired her.

"You are truly a vision," he finally said, his attention still on her breasts. A smile tugged at the corner of his mouth when he noticed what she had tucked inside her bra.

He moved closer and boldly reached behind her back, unhooking her bra with the ease of an experienced lover. The smile on his face grew as he caught the lacy apparel before it hit the floor, and the condom that she'd stuck into her C cup.

Dexter let the garment drop from his hand, but he held the foil packet up. "Looks like you came prepared."

Her gorgeous lips twitched in an effort to keep from smiling, and she shrugged. "I figured just in case."

"Well, we shouldn't let this go to waste." He set the condom on the side table, aware of her gaze following his every move. Watching her watch him was a serious turn-on.

He reached for the tail of his T-shirt, and effortlessly lifted it over his head, adding it to the slow-growing pile of clothes. He didn't waste any time shedding his sweats and socks.

With every piece of clothing he removed, he could sense her increased arousal, turning him on even more. Heat rose to her cheeks and she swallowed hard as her gaze took in his naked body, making him glad that he never slacked on his rigorous workouts.

"I knew you had a nice body, but this…"

The reserved woman was suddenly replaced by one bold enough to kick off her heels and step to him. Mona inched her small hands up his torso, and the tips of her luscious breasts grazed the thin hairs on his chest. A tremble ran through Dexter and the electric current surging from her body to his had him ready to leap out of his skin.

He fought to control the intense need to take her quickly against the wall. He wanted her more than he had desired anything in a long time, but he also wanted this night to be special. For the both of them.

No, he wouldn't rush through this. He'd take his time and love her the way she deserved to be loved.

Needing to feel all of her against him, he snaked his arms around her and palmed her butt, bringing her flush against his body. An overwhelming feeling of possession gripped him and he knew right then that he would do whatever it took to hang onto her. No way would he let her ex or his past sins keep him from spending the rest of his life with this woman.

He claimed her lips, devouring them as he kneaded her bottom, grinding against her with a hunger he felt to his core. All thoughts of confessing his sins flew from his mind when she moaned into his mouth. He had to have her.

Now.

Mona gasped. "Dexter!" Flustered, she grabbed onto his upper arms when he suddenly lifted her, his fingers gripping the back of her thighs as he set her on the bed.

Adrenaline was pumping so hard through his body, he felt like he was about to explode.

"I need you," he mumbled against her scented neck. Nipping. Licking. And loving the little sounds she was making.

"I need you, too," she said breathily. "But…"

She wiggled out of his hold and started to slide her panties off, but he stopped her with a hand on her arm.

"Let me."

A slow, shy grin covered her mouth and she sat back on her elbows, giving him a complete view of all that awaited him once he slid the red strap of material down her shapely legs.

God, this woman. His shaft pulsed with need.

Don't rush this, he reminded himself.

Dexter stared down at her semi-naked form, taking in her more-than-a-handful breasts and nipples that were begging to be sucked. His gaze moved lower, to the strap of material covering the apex between her thighs, and his erection grew harder.

He looked up to find Mona's worried gaze on him.

"Damn, woman. Your body is a work of art," he said, meaning every word, and she visibly relaxed.

He dragged his hand down the center of her body, appreciating the softness of her skin and taking in every dimple, every muscle, and each one of her curves. His inspection, and his hand, didn't stop until he reached the top of her panties.

She lifted slightly and he slowly slid down the red lace and let it fall to the floor.

Dexter steadied himself, mentally preparing to enjoy every inch of her tempting body.

Mona sucked in a breath and a shiver skirted up her spine when Dexter lifted her leg.

"Dex," she said on a shaky breath when his mouth touched the inside of her ankle. Tingles of pleasure shot from the soles of her feet to the top of her head.

Her head fell against a pillow and she fisted the sheets, biting down on her bottom lip to keep from whimpering. Dexter planted feathery kisses on the inside of her calf, and worked his way up her thigh.

Mona's eyes drifted closed while she enjoyed his journey.

Each touch of his mouth on her heated skin felt so good, but as his soft kisses moved further up her other leg and then to the top of her inner thigh, her body tensed.

As if sensing her discomfort, Dexter lifted his head, his gaze meeting hers. "What's wrong?"

She closed her eyes tightly, knowing she was about to ruin the most intimate moment she'd ever had with a man. She wanted him more than anything. Why...

"Hey." He climbed onto the bed next to her. "We don't have to do this if you're not ready."

"I'm ready," she blurted, forcing herself to look at him. "I want this. I want you more than anything. But..."

"But what?" His large hand rested on her stomach. The way he caressed her with such love and the tenderness gleaming in his eyes, stirred something within her. What was it about this man that could ignite her feminine juices with a look, or a simple touch?

"Sweetheart. If—"

"I want us to be together, but I don't want to do what I think you were about to do."

After a slight hesitation, realization shown on his face and he nodded. His intense gaze studied her as if reading her mind.

She didn't want to tell him that she had never had oral sex, but by the sympathy in his eyes, it was pretty safe to say he had figured it out.

"My job is to please you, Mona," he said, the deep rumble of his voice washing over her like a gentle caress. "If ever I do anything that makes you uncomfortable, tell me."

His words almost brought tears to her eyes. In her world, sex had always been about pleasing Russell, not the other way around. But again…he wasn't Russell.

"Do you want us to stop?"

"Absolutely not," she said quickly.

A slow smile spread across his mouth and then he laughed. "Good, because I want you too bad to stop. Come here."

He pulled her on top of him as if she were as light as a feather.

"Just so that we're clear. I'm not going to ask you to do anything you're not comfortable with, but I plan to make love to every inch of your body. Maybe not all in one night, but before long, you're going to want to feel my mouth *all* over you. You're going to experience what it's like for a man to worship your sweet a—"

Mona smothered his last words with a heated kiss, wanting to show him just how much she wanted him. She might not be ready for oral sex, but she was definitely ready to have him buried deep inside of her.

Feeling his length growing beneath her, she yanked her mouth from his and grabbed the condom, handing it to him.

"Not yet," he said tossing it to the pillow beside them. Without warning, he flipped her onto her back. "There's something I've wanted to do since the moment you stripped out of your dress."

His large hands cupped her breasts, gently squeezing them before pulling one of the pebbled nipples into his mouth. Pleasure pulsed through Mona's veins. Her eyes drifted shut and her body hummed, loving the way his tongue licked and twirled around her hardened peaks.

"Mmm," Dexter murmured and moved lower, his lips searing a tantalizing path down her ribs to her stomach. "You smell so damn good, everywhere I kiss you."

As his hands explored, touched, and squeezed, his mouth followed over her heated flesh with those same feathery kisses from earlier.

For weeks Mona had wondered if their relationship would progress to this level. Now, she didn't know how much more of the delicious torture from his exploring hands or experienced lips she could take.

Aroused beyond belief, she ached against him. "Now, Dex." That was all she had to say for him to slowly lift his head and flash that devilish grin.

"Whatever you want, sweetheart."

He reached over to the other side of the bed and grabbed the foil packet, and quickly sheathed himself. Nudging her thighs apart, he hovered above her before claiming her lips and kissing her tenderly.

Mona drew in a breath as his thick shaft teased her opening. A sizzling sensation soared through her, like hot lava flowing down the sides of a volcano. Her hips moved on their own accord, bucking against him, needing him inside her.

"De—Dexter," she said on an unsteady breath, her nails digging into his large biceps. He eased into her tightness inch by inch, burying himself to the hilt as she adjusted around his length.

"Ah, baby," he groaned close to her ear as he settled in and started rotating his hips. "You feel so good."

Their bodies moved in perfect sync as he slid in and out of her, picking up pace with each thrust. He lifted her hips from the bed, as he plunged deeper.

Mona's body temperature rose to a fiery level, making her squirm beneath him. Waves of ecstasy lapped at every cell in her body, pushing her that much closer to the edge of her control.

A surge of heat swept through Dexter like a roaring flame and his grip on her hips tightened when she clenched around his shaft. He cursed under his breath and gritted his teeth, as his body moved on its own accord and his impending release grew near. He didn't know how much longer he could hold on, but…

"D—Dex," Mona panted over and over with each thrust, spurring him to go deeper and harder, his body growing taut each time he plunged into her.

"Oh my G…" she screamed suddenly, jerking violently against him. Dexter held on tight as her nails dug into his arm and seconds later, his ferocious release followed right behind hers. Then they collapsed against the pillows, panting.

His heart raced fast enough to beat right out of his chest while he tried catching his breath. But he wanted more. Much more.

They lay there for a moment. Their ragged breathing was the only sounds in the quietness of the bedroom.

"I knew we'd be amazing together, but damn. After that, I don't think I'll ever be able to get enough of you."

Mona glanced up at him with a satisfied smile. "I feel the same about you. We should do that again…but I want to be on top."

Dexter threw his head back and laughed. "Anything you want. Just give me a few minutes to recuperate."

Hours later, Dexter held a sleeping Mona in his arms as he stared up at the ceiling. Her ex was an even bigger asshole than he had originally thought. How could he have an incredible woman like her and not cherish her? And not love on her the way she deserved to be loved?

Then again, he was just as much of an asshole. He still hadn't told her about the accident, and now that he'd slept with her, he had no idea how to start the conversation. But he wanted her to know everything. No secrets.

Tomorrow. I'll tell her tomorrow.

Chapter Twelve

Mona jogged over the rough terrain to catch up with Dexter. They had hiked three miles already and her feet hurt, her back ached a little, but she couldn't think of another time that she'd had this much fun. Being one with nature was exhilarating. Or maybe getting some good loving the night before and that morning had a way of making a woman feel like she could conquer the world.

"We have at least a mile to go. Are you sure you can make it back? I can carry you if you like," Dexter said seriously, and Mona burst out laughing.

"There is no way I'm letting you carry me anywhere." Sometimes she wondered if he forgot how old he was. Of course, she didn't voice that sentiment, for fear of him trying to prove he could carry her the distance.

At first, he frowned, but then he shook his head and shrugged. "Fine, but don't say I didn't offer." He kept moving down the hill and she slipped her hand into his.

"Thanks for the offer, but I'm fine."

They continued walking, both caught up in their own thoughts. Peace settled around her as birds chirped nearby, and a gentle breeze caressed her cheeks. Not being an outdoors type person, Mona hadn't known what to expect, but spending time in the open air was freeing, as well as relaxing.

If some of her former friends in New York saw her now, they probably wouldn't recognize her wearing an insulated jacket, worn jeans, and hiking boots.

Dexter squeezed her gloved hand. "Let's stop for a minute." He guided her off the main path and to an oak tree. The wind had picked up and she zipped her coat up higher.

Dexter set the backpack on the ground and pulled her close.

"Your nose and cheeks are rosy." He placed a kiss on the tip of her nose and she nestled closer, wrapping her arms around his waist. Her face might be a little cold, but being near him had her on fire from the top of her head to the soles of her feet, even more so when he lowered his head and captured her lips in a heated kiss. Cupping her face between his large hands, he deepened their connection.

Each day with him highlighted how perfect they were together. For a person who wasn't looking for anything serious, she had certainly hit the jackpot. She couldn't see herself with anyone else. Some moments that realization scared her to death, but right now, all she could think about was doing more with Dexter than kissing.

Talking and laughing coming from the distance had them slowly pulling apart.

Dexter stared into her eyes before a smile lifted the corner of his glorious mouth. "Kissing you has definitely become my favorite pastime."

Mona grinned, joy singing through her veins. "Mine too. I think we should do it as often as possible."

"I agree. That idea will go great with what I have planned for this evening." He wiggled his eyebrows, making her laugh. "Let's drink a little water and keep it moving."

Once they returned to the trail, they walked side by side, and conversation flowed easily.

"I'm thinking that once we get to the condo, you can take a long, warm bubble bath to work out any soreness," Dexter said.

"Who said I was sore?"

"The wincing every so often kind of gave you away." He smiled and wrapped his arm around her shoulder, placing a kiss on her forehead. "You'll be good as new. Then we can order Chinese food and camp out in front of the TV and maybe watch a couple of movies."

"Sounds wonderful."

"Have you reconsidered your stance on marriage?" Dexter asked out of the blue, and took the lead as they walked down a steep hill.

Mona hadn't necessarily thought about marriage, but there hadn't been a day since she and Dexter started hanging out that she didn't think about him. Yet, giving up her independence to live with a man again wasn't something she was in a hurry to do. Then again, she already knew living with him would be totally different than living with Russell.

"I'll take your silence as a no," Dexter said, jarring Mona out of her thoughts.

"I know you're looking to get married again, Dex, but I like my newfound freedom."

"Does that mean you're still dating other men?"

"No," she said quickly. "I told you that you're the only man I'm seeing." The only man she wanted to see, she thought, but didn't add.

"But you're not interested in a formal commitment."

Mona sighed wishing he would change the subject. "Dex...I like things the way they are between us. We've been having a wonderful time. We don't need a formal commitment."

"What if I told you I wanted more?"

"More like what?" she asked carefully, not sure she really wanted to know the answer.

He stopped abruptly and turned, forcing her to pull up short. "I want you, Mona. *All* of you."

*

When Mona didn't respond, Dexter gave her a quick kiss on the lips and started back down the trail. He wanted more than anything to tell her that he had fallen in love with her, but she wasn't ready. During the time they'd spent together, growing closer, he thought their feelings for each other were in line.

Apparently not.

Knowing that kept him from telling her more about his past. It had already been hard confessing his drinking problem, but before he would share his deepest secret, he had to know where her head was at. He had to know she was committed to moving forward with him and taking their relationship to the next level. He was a traditional guy. Dating to be dating wasn't him. Once he found the right woman, he wanted to marry and build a life with her. Mona was that woman. He just had to wait until she knew it too.

She caught up and walked alongside him, despite the narrow path.

"Please don't be mad at me. For all of my adult life, I was with a man who I always catered to. Making sure all of his needs were taken care of, from ensuring meals were on the table on time to managing the household budget. I took care of him and our home, as well as traveled with him on business. Basically, I did what I assume most wives do—I supported my man."

Dexter listened. Considering how she had given of herself in her previous relationship, he wondered what Russell did for her. Surely, she didn't stick around just for the man's wealth and luxury. She wasn't that type of woman, at least not the woman he'd grown to love.

"For the first time in my life, I'm able to put myself first. Do what I want and…be who I want to be."

"And you don't think you can do that in a committed relationship? You don't think you can be who you are with me?"

She released a dramatic sigh. "This is not coming out right. Basically, Dex. I don't want to take care of a man again."

Dexter slowed. "Sweetheart, I can take care of myself. I don't know what all Russell expected of you, but all I would want from you in a relationship is your love and respect. That's it."

She stopped and looked at him with confusion. "Then what's the point of marriage if I don't take care of you and our home?"

Dexter was slowly starting to understand the power Russell had had over her. "Mona, marriage is not only about taking care of the other person. It's a partnership. I would never expect my wife to be the sole cook, cleaner, breadwinner or anything like that. I want to remarry because I want to grow old with a woman by my side who I love spending time with, enjoying the rest of this life I have left."

"I see."

"Do you really? I understand marriage is different for everyone, but so that we're clear, what you described is not what I'm looking for. I love the relationship that you and I are building. We're a heck of a team, balancing each other in everything we've done together. That's what I want. Someone to *share* my life with. Not someone to do everything for me."

For the first time in the last few minutes, she smiled up at him. "We do make a pretty good team, don't we?"

"We do." He pulled her into a bear hug. "We make a helluva team. You let me know when you're ready to take this team to the next level."

Chapter Thirteen

Mona sat at the dining room table of the Jenkins family home, sipping a steaming cup of coffee. Steven and Katherine Jenkins, the founders of Jenkins & Sons Construction, held a family brunch at their estate every Sunday. Mona had attended a few times, but two things were always guaranteed when around the Jenkins family: good food and plenty of laughs. Today was no different.

Sitting next to Sumeera as she, Toni, and Martina discussed everything from work to the latest Hollywood scandal kept her entertained.

"Soon, Hollywood will only be comprised of women. With all of the allegations of sexual assault coming to the forefront, women will be ruling the entertainment world," Toni said. She had on her usual attire, jeans and a sassy T-shirt about plumbers. Today's shirt read: *The sexiest plumber you'll ever meet.*

"Women rule the world in every other aspect. They might as well take over Hollywood, too," Martina added while sipping from a glass of white wine, reminding Mona that she hadn't had a drink since her first date with Dexter. Surprisingly, she hadn't missed alcohol. "Now maybe we'll get more male nudity on the big screen. I'm sick of always seeing a woman's tits and bare ass while the guy is fully clothed."

"MJ, only you would say something like that," Sumeera said, shaking her head. "What do you think, Mom?"

Surprised by the question, Mona thought about her response before speaking. "Actually, I think Martina is right. There is definitely an imbalance of gender nudity on TV and in movies. Though personally, I could do without all of it on the big screen, but Martina has a good point."

"What stupid stuff is MJ spewing now?" Christina asked, carrying a plate loaded with food. "Hey, everybody. What I miss?"

"Well, hello to you too, cuz." Martina bumped shoulders with Christina when she sat in the seat next to her. "Mona was just agreeing with me about sex."

Her eyes bulged while the others at the table laughed.

"Don't worry, Mona. I don't believe a word she says," Christina said, still laughing.

"I didn't know you were back in town." Martina poured Christina a glass of wine. "Don't you look refreshed. I guess the thug lawyer put it on you real good while you guys were on vacation."

Mona hadn't heard the story of why Martina referred to Christina's husband, Luke, as the thug lawyer. He had moved from New York to Cincinnati a few years ago where he was a defense attorney. Now he worked with Christina's uncle, Ben, at his law firm. Luke definitely had swag, but by no means did he come across as a thug.

"You're damn near glowing," Martina continued, narrowing her eyes at Christina. "Wait. Unless—"

"Don't even go there, MJ." Christina shoveled a heap of salad into her mouth, then pointed her fork at each of her cousins. "I'm leaving the baby-making to you guys." Though her plate was full, she'd only loaded it up with vegetarian dishes. "Speaking of babies. Where are the kids?"

"With their fathers," Toni said, and put a forkful of carrot cake into her mouth. Mona didn't know how they all stayed so fit, yet had huge appetites. She couldn't eat another thing even if she wanted to.

"Since we're on clean-up duty this week, we thought it only fair that the daddies be on kid duty."

"Speaking of glowing. So, Mona. You and Dex, huh?" Toni said between bites.

"Yeah, Mom. I did notice a little more pep in your step. What gives?"

"Is it true that even though there's snow on the roof, there's still fire in the furnace?" Martina asked.

Mona's mouth dropped opened, and heat flooded her cheeks.

"You don't have to answer, Mona, but inquiring minds want to know," Toni said laughing.

"A lady never tells," Mona said, with as much priss in her voice as she could muster.

"Well, I'm no lady. When I become a senior citizen—"

"Hey! We are not senior citizens yet." Mona couldn't help but join in with their laughter. Instead of going to the sunroom with some of the other women closer to her age, she had opted to hang out with Sumeera. She and Dexter had eaten together, but after he finished, he headed to the lower level to play dominoes with some of the guys.

"Well, I think it's great Mona and Dex are dating. He's a good guy," Christina said and poured herself a glass of water from the pitcher on the table. "I'm glad he's gotten his life back together. It was too bad Peyton had to fire him," Christina said of her sister who used to run the company. "I'm glad you didn't hold the accident against him. It was—"

"What accident?" Mona asked. Dexter hadn't mentioned being fired from Jenkins & Sons Construction. Nor did he tell her anything about an accident.

Silence filled the room before Sumeera spoke. "He didn't tell you?"

"No, he never mentioned an accident. What happened?"

Unease spread through her body as she looked from one to the other.

"I'm sorry. I shouldn't have brought it up," Christina apologized.

"Why won't one of you just tell me what happened?"

Martina shook her head. "Normally, I'd be all about spreading somebody in this family's business, but in this case... That's Dexter's story to tell."

Mona's stomach stirred with trepidation. Martina had a reputation in the family of saying whatever was on her mind, not caring whose feelings got hurt. For her to refuse to share Dexter's story said a lot.

Whatever happened must have been bad. Very bad.

*

"Fever in the funkhouse!" Ben Sr. yelled as he slammed the domino on the card table.

"Dang, Dad. Say it, don't spray it." Ben, Jr., also known as BJ, wiped his face with his forearm.

Dexter laughed along with everyone else and they all started talking at once. As usual, when they got together for a game of dominoes, there was more trash-talking in that small room than on a public basketball court. Four guys sat at the table and two others on the sideline, but it sounded more like twenty.

"Any day now, old man. It's your turn," Nick said to Dexter. He was sitting to his left and had Chanelle sitting contently on his lap.

"Watch it with the old-man crack, young blood. Remember, I used to change your diapers."

"Hence...old man," Ben Jr. cracked and they all laughed again.

"All right. Whatchu got to say about this? Fifteen stitches for your britches!" Dexter slammed down the tile.

"Motherfu—"

"Watch your mouth, boy. There's a kid in the room," Ben said to his son.

"Really? She can't even talk."

"Still..." Nick added, and again the room exploded with more trash talk.

This is what Dexter had missed during the years he had stayed clear of most of the family. Sunday brunch was a time for several generations of Jenkins relatives to come together and enjoy each other's company over food, laughter, and a host of other activities.

The estate was so big, it was easy for fifty people to be in the home and not feel crowded. Some hung out on the first floor, mostly the women. While the guys occupied the lower level, consisting of two game rooms, the small one that Dexter was currently in, and a larger one that held a pool table and a few other games, as well as a bar. Most of the older men hung out in the lounge area, which was referred to as the man cave.

Dexter looked up and saw Mona standing near the entrance to the small room. He smiled at her, but when she didn't return the smile, he set his tiles face down on the table and stood.

"Give me a second, guys. I'll be right back." Dexter crossed the room. "Hey. Everything all right?" He placed a quick kiss on her lips.

"Do you mind if we leave?" she asked and glanced around, rubbing her hands up and down her folded arms as if she were cold despite the sweater she had on.

"Sure. We can head out, but is something wrong? Are you feeling okay?" He wrapped his arm around her waist and felt her stiffen before she relaxed.

"I think it's time for us to go."

He stared down at her until she actually looked at him. Seemed he wouldn't find out what was wrong until they left.

"Jerry, can you finish up my hand?" he asked another one of Steven's grandsons.

Jerry rubbed his hands together and grinned. "With pleasure."

Holding Mona's hand, something that was second nature now, Dexter led her up the stairs, wondering what had happened. When they reached the top landing, they ran into Sumeera.

"You guys leaving?"

"Yeah, your mom's ready to go."

Sumeera nodded. "Okay. Mom, give me a call later," she said, and they hugged. Then Sumeera surprised Dexter with a tight hug. "Be honest with her. Everything will be fine," she whispered, and Dexter's whole body went on alert.

Be honest with her.

Alarm hammered inside his chest as the words played over and over in his head. While he and Mona walked to his truck, all types of thoughts clogged his mind. Either Mona knew about the accident or someone hinted about it.

Whichever it was, Dexter only had himself to blame if she no longer trusted him. Or no longer wanted to be with him. He had wanted to tell her the other night, but once she removed her dress, all other thoughts vanished. Then during their hiking trip, he had thought about talking to her about the accident, but selfishly didn't want to ruin their perfect day. And then there was last night. A night that was much like the night before, with them sharing his bed and him falling deeper in love with her.

He helped Mona into the truck and then climbed into the driver's side. He stuck his key into the ignition and then dropped his head against the seat.

How the hell was he supposed to start this conversation?

"Tell me about the accident."

Dexter swallowed, his pulse pounding in his ear. "Okay, but not here."

Chapter Fourteen

Dexter appreciated Mona's willingness to wait to discuss the accident until they were in the comfort of her living room. It also gave him time to prepare himself for whatever came next for them.

The Bible might say the truth will set you free, but if there was any way around sharing the secrets of his past with her, he would take it. He had made peace with all of those involved in the accident years ago, but not knowing what her reaction would be once he told her everything had him on edge.

Falling in love with her had happened quickly, but there was no way their relationship could progress if he wasn't totally honest. He didn't want to lose the woman who had given him hope in finding love again.

"Here you go," Mona said, handing Dexter a large mug of steaming black coffee. The scent of French vanilla wafted to his nose and he inhaled.

"Thanks."

"You're welcome." She sat on the sofa next to him. For the majority of the drive to the condo, conversation mainly centered on the Jenkins family and the brunch.

"Are you ready to talk?" she asked, sitting back and crossing one leg over the other. The light-pink sweater she wore highlighted her dark skin and made her look soft and feminine. The top was paired with fitted blue jeans, something she'd been wearing more often.

Dexter's heart squeezed with love. She was the kindest person he knew and she deserved someone better than him. But he couldn't give her up. He didn't want to lose her. She was a part of him.

God, this woman…

"I don't know if I would've ever been ready to share the part of my life that I'm most ashamed of had you not confronted me. You mean the world to me, Mona. I never want to disappoint you, but…"

She leaned forward and touched his forearm. "Tell me. Whatever happened, I'm the last person who will judge you. Like you told me over a month ago, we all have things in our past that we're not proud of or wish we could have a do-over."

Dexter set his coffee on the table, and placed his elbows on his thighs. "I had been stationed in Georgia when I retired from the army, but Lillie and I agreed we didn't want to live in the south. We moved back to Cincinnati, which is where we grew up, and I started working construction at Jenkins & Sons. I enjoyed the work for many years."

"What changed?"

Dexter's throat tightened against the foreboding swirling inside of him, and he swallowed several times before continuing.

"It wasn't unusual for me and a couple of guys to go out for a drink after work," he finally said. "But then one or two beers started turning into three and four a night. I never recalled being sloppy-drunk, but my ex-wife called me out on my excessive drinking. So I slowed down."

Dexter ran his hand over his mouth and down his chin, guilt and embarrassment rested in his chest. He might've finally forgiven himself and moved on, but it was never easy to think about, or discuss this devastating event.

"Dexter," Mona said quietly, jarring him enough with that single word to get out of his head and continue.

"I still had a couple of beers every night. However, instead of going out, I'd drink at home. One night I attended a friend's birthday party and had way too much alcohol. The next morning, I got up as usual feeling fine, but during lunch…" he cleared his throat, "I had a couple more drinks."

Mona moved closer and rubbed a hand in a circular motion on his back, sensing the emotion swelling within him.

"As a crane operator I dealt with heavy machinery and that afternoon, I did so while intoxicated."

Mona's hand froze. She didn't say anything, but Dexter could feel the tension…and fear seeping through her pores.

Just say it. Just rip the bandage off and tell her.

"I was lifting a roof-top air-conditioning unit and lost control. It dropped five stories. The unit barely missed several workers on the ground and…critically injured another."

Mona's hand went to her mouth and tears filled her eyes. "Oh, Dexter."

"I almost killed a man, Mona. He almost died because of me. A young husband and…father of three. He'll always be disabled…because of me," Dexter choked out.

He shook his head and wrapped both hands around his coffee mug. He was shaking too badly to lift it from the table, so he left it. Instead, he stood and moved to a nearby window, struggling to catch his breath. It was as if someone had their hands around his neck and was applying pressure little by little, squeezing his windpipe and hindering air flow.

After a long moment, he continued. "My recklessness sabotaged a job and ruined several lives that day. I was arrested and charged with reckless endangerment. Thankfully, I only received probation and a hefty fine. It could've been so much worse. Had my coworker died, I could've been charged with involuntary…manslaughter."

Dexter ran his hands down his face. Discussing that time in his life was like reliving a nightmare he couldn't wake from.

"I lost my job and cost Jenkins & Sons a ton of money. The project was shut down during a lengthy investigation, meaning most of the guys on that assignment had forced leave; the air-conditioning unit cost tens of thousands; and God only knows how many safety violations were incurred. Not to mention the lawsuit from the victim's family. If the company hadn't had a solid foundation, I could've caused one of the best construction companies in the state to close its doors."

Terrible regrets consumed him as he finally turned to face her. Not surprisingly, Mona sat stunned, with her hand over her mouth and eyes filled with tears. She had to think he was the lowest form of human life to do something so stupid.

Dexter swallowed the despair in his throat and gazed back out the window, not looking at anything particular. Minutes ticked by as he got his own emotions under control, and then Mona wrapped her arms around his midsection.

"I'm so sorry. That had to be awful for you. I can't even imagine how hard that had to be for everyone involved."

"It was the worse day of my life."

"Come and sit down."

Mona slipped her arm through his and escorted him across the room. They reclaimed their seats. Though his coffee had cooled some, it was still warm enough as he took a sip.

At first, shortly after the incident, Dexter swept in and out of drunkenness for a few months. He hadn't even known he was an alcoholic until the drinking got worse and his wife insisted he go to rehab. He explained that to Mona. He had pulled himself together, but it had only lasted six months before he was back to drinking.

More guilt seeped into his soul. "Lillie is one of the most loving people I know. She gave me more chances than I deserved. Until she couldn't take it any longer. She told me that either I moved out, or she would. I left."

Mona sat stiffly beside him and remained quiet.

"No way would I expect her to leave when I was the one who couldn't get my act together. We talked often, but things weren't the same between us. I knew it and so did she. Too much had happened. Months later, she filed for divorce. She told me if I didn't love myself enough to stop drinking, then there wasn't much else she could do."

"How long did you have a drinking problem?"

"I will always have a drinking problem, Mona, but I've learned to control the urges. After the divorce, I got sober for a year and thought one drink wouldn't hurt." He shook his head. "I was wrong. I didn't get drunk, but while I was home one evening, I had a couple of beers. I figured a beer every now and then would be okay. That I could stop whenever I wanted. Problem was, I always wanted another one."

"Why'd you even risk having a drink after being sober?"

He shrugged. "I thought I could control it. That I could choose to stop drinking whenever I wanted. Some might not believe alcoholism is a disease, but for me, I think it is. I've made peace with the fact that I'll never be able to consume a beer or a glass of scotch, and not want another and then another. That's a fact that I will always have to live with."

Mona asked a few more questions and Dexter answered as honestly as he could. After about twenty minutes of discussing his marriage, alcoholism, and his children, silence fell between them.

She stood and carried her mug to the kitchen. "I wish you would've told me this sooner," she said, looking at him from behind the breakfast bar.

He had never wanted to see disappointment in her eyes. During the conversation, she had listened and didn't seem to judge him, but that didn't mean she wanted to keep seeing him.

"Mona…you mean the world to me. Please don't let my past mistake come between us. I wanted to tell you. At first, I wanted to wait until we knew each other better. Then when we started getting closer, it never seemed to be the right time to tell you. And then I fell in love with you. *I. Love. You.*"

She rubbed her temples. "Don't. Don't say that."

Dexter walked across the room and stood on the other side of the counter. "It's true. I've known for a while, but the other day when I walked Russell out, the realization of how much I loved you hit me hard. He told me I wasn't good enough for you. That I would never be able to provide you with the life you're accustomed to. I'll admit, that was tough to hear."

It had been a long time since he had felt that low…and unworthy. Knowing he had crippled a man, and could have killed others because of drinking, often made him question his worth. But that was his past. He made a horrible mistake, but he deserved a chance to get his life right. He deserved a chance at happiness, and Mona made him happy.

"Though I knew we couldn't move forward until I told you, I didn't know how. I found every excuse, telling myself that I was waiting for the right time." Desperateness tore at his heart. "I don't want to lose you, Mona. I'll do whatever it takes to prove to you that I'm worthy of you."

"Oh, Dexter." She swiped quickly at a few tears that fell to her cheeks. "I—I don't know what to say. This is a lot to take in."

He reached across the counter and held her hand. "I know, and I'm so sorry…for everything." Dexter released her. "I'll go, but I hope this isn't the end for us."

He turned and walked out, feeling as if he was leaving behind a part of himself. He couldn't help but wonder if this would be the last time he'd see her. He had foolishly thought that he would eventually be able to have all that he once had with Lillie and more. And what he wanted more than anything was to have Mona in his life forever.

Dexter had no intentions of ever allowing alcohol to derail his life again. He also wanted an opportunity to show her they could have a wonderful life together.

All I need is a chance.

Chapter Fifteen

"I was thinking you can put two dressing rooms in this area." Sumeera pointed to the corner in the back of the potential space for the boutique. Mona had been following her around the oversize area for the past twenty minutes trying to envision the set-up.

"I don't know, Sumeera. This store is bigger than I was thinking."

"I know, Mom. Weren't you listening to me?" she asked, frowning. "When we first arrived, I told you Liam is proposing that the space be divided into two smaller stores," she said, referring to Nick's cousin, an architect.

"Oh." Mona ran her hands through her hair, exhaustion getting the best of her. She had tossed and turned for the last three nights and was paying for the lack of sleep. Every few minutes, thoughts of Dexter filtered into her mind. She was still troubled by his admission, but more than that, she wondered how he was doing.

Her cell phone rang for the second time in five minutes. She knew it wasn't Dexter because the week before, they had been playing around with their phones and he had suggested specific ring tones for them. The deal was they chose each other's ring tone. He had picked "When Love Calls" for her phone, and she had chosen "I've Had the Time of My Life" for his.

"Are you going to keep avoiding Dexter?" Sumeera said when Mona didn't answer her phone.

"It's not him."

Her daughter stared at her, as if waiting for her to continue, and then the phone rang again.

"If it's not him, then who are you avoid..." Her words trailed off and her eyes narrowed. "Russell? Really, Mom?" Sumeera had long since stopped calling her father Dad. "You're still keeping in contact with him?"

"No, but...he's been calling me." No way was she telling her about his visit.

"Then block his number. You don't have to tolerate him harassing you. Unless..." Sumeera huffed out a breath. "Please tell me you're not getting back together with him."

"Of course not. We're history."

"Then why haven't you cut him loose? There's no reason for him to keep calling you."

"Your father has depended on me for pretty much everything for so many years, he's having a hard time moving on."

"That's not your problem. Make him understand that you guys are over. Tell him to stop calling. You don't have to accept his inability to move on."

"Until today, I hadn't heard from him in days, but you're right. I need to stop avoiding his calls and tell him...better yet, I'll block his number right now."

While Mona was doing that, Sumeera's cell phone rang. She glanced at the screen.

"I'm sorry, Mom, but I need to take this." She answered the phone and moved to the far side of the store.

Mona couldn't hear her and was glad for the reprieve. She stepped to the large windows overlooking the parking lot, and Dexter immediately came to mind.

Listening to his confession about the horrific accident, the way he had shared such an emotional incident, had been heartbreaking. She couldn't imagine living with the responsibility of harming so many people on her conscience. He said he had made peace with the accident and had asked forgiveness from everyone involved, something that was a part of the twelve-step program of Alcoholics Anonymous. But all Mona could think about was what if it happened again.

I will always have a drinking problem.

His words rattled around in her mind. What was she supposed to do with that? If drinking would always be a problem for him, then that meant he could slip up at any time. Meaning more accidents could happen. The next time he might not be as lucky.

His other revelation had been equally shocking.

I love you.

Though she felt the same way, Mona hadn't expected his declaration and hadn't been ready to express her feelings for him. She was in love with him, and wasn't sure when it happened. All she knew was that, though she didn't want to be tied down again, she couldn't imagine not having him in her life.

"Considering how distracted you've been today, are you sure you don't want to talk about Dexter?" Sumeera asked, returning from her call.

Caught up in her thoughts, Mona hadn't realized she had been standing behind her.

"Why won't you talk about him? Tell me how you're feeling about the whole thing."

Mona's gut churned with despair as she fought back tears. "I feel like I lost my best friend," she choked out, her heart crumbling a little more. It had been days since she'd seen Dexter, but it felt like weeks. She already missed him.

"Wait. You broke up with him?"

Mona shook her head and reined in her emotions. "Not officially, but I'm planning to tell him that we're done."

That morning, she had made the decision not to see him again, which was probably why her heart ached. Living in the same building, she was bound to run into him, but knowing they would no longer spend time together felt like a knife to the chest.

"Why? That incident at J&S happened years ago. Dex had been in a bad place when he *used* to drink. More importantly, it was an accident."

"He had been drinking on the job, Sumeera. What if he had killed that guy?"

"But he didn't."

"But he could have. The man's foot was crushed. He will never walk right again. I can't even imagine the emotional toll he's endured since then. What if I trust Dexter to never drink again, but he ends up drunk one day?" Mona swiped at an errant tear. "What if he actually kills someone next time? What if—"

"Mom, we all live with *what-ifs* all the time. If we let the unknown stop us from doing what we wanted to do, what we're destined to do, we would never accomplish anything. None of us know what the future holds, but if you care about Dexter…or if you love him like I think you do, don't give up on him. He knows what it feels like to lose everything. He won't want to risk drinking again."

"I want a stress-free, carefree, no-responsibility relationship. Hooking up with an alcoholic is not what I envisioned for myself. If Dexter happens to start drinking again, start making poor choices, some of that will fall on me. I don't think I can handle another man who is so dependent on me."

Sumeera frowned. "Dexter is not Russell, Mom. He's not needy and selfish. He can take care of himself *and* you, for that matter. He's been doing it for years. Dexter is a wonderful guy who made some bad choices and has committed several years to turning his life around. I get that you're concerned that he might slip up. It can happen, but what if he never does? What if he remains sober for the rest of his life and you miss out on the best thing that's ever happened to you because you're afraid to take a chance?

"Don't hold his past against him, thinking that he'll make the same mistakes. Give him a chance to prove to you that he can be the man you deserve."

Mona mulled over her daughter's words. Dexter hadn't held her past against her. The way she had abandoned her daughter. Putting a man's needs before her own child was criminal. Yet, he hadn't walked away from her. Even Sumeera had given her another chance to get it right. A chance for them to have the type of mother-daughter relationship Mona had longed for.

Why couldn't she do the same for Dexter?

She glanced away from Sumeera's intent gaze and thought about what she'd be giving up if she walked away from him. How many times had she said that this was a new chapter in her life, a chance for new experiences? In the short time of knowing Dexter, he'd done that for her. He had unleashed a passion within her that she had thought long gone.

Mona moved around the room as she recalled all that she loved about him. She loved spending time with him. His thoughtfulness and those sweet kisses always gave her something to look forward to.

How could she walk away from him? He was the man she had fallen in love with.

"And as for being in a committed relationship and possibly marriage in the future," Sumeera continued, "technically, you and Dexter are already committed. I still don't understand your feelings regarding marriage, but just because it didn't happen for you with Russell, doesn't mean you should give up the idea. Spending the rest of your life with Dexter will be way different than the first half of your life with my father."

"You're right...about all of it. I can't give up on Dexter all because I fear the unknown. Besides...I miss him so much," she said, a heaviness in her chest. "Until the other morning, I didn't realize how much I've come to count on him being around. It's been weird not sitting across from him at breakfast."

"Love has that effect on people."

"I didn't say I lo—"

"You didn't have to. Whenever you talk about Dex, your whole face lights up. And I saw the way you two looked at each other at brunch. I wasn't the only one who noticed." Sumeera smiled. "It's nice to see you happy, Mom. Life is short. If Dexter makes you happy, don't let him get away. Like in everything, there will be ups and down, but see where the relationship goes. Enjoy the ride and don't get so caught up with the what-ifs."

Mona smiled for the first time in days, feeling encouraged. She didn't know what the future held, but she looked forward to finding out…with Dexter by her side.

She glanced at her watch, trying to determine what he might be doing at the moment. Normally, he finished up his workday by six, which was in about an hour. Maybe she could invite him over so they could talk.

"So, what do you think?"

"I think I want to see what the future holds for me and Dexter."

Sumeera flashed a knowing smile. "Actually, I meant, what do you think about the store? Can you see having the boutique here?"

"Yes, I can, but I'd like for Dexter to see the place before I make any decisions. I want to get his opinion."

Apprehension rumbled through her. She had no idea what she'd say to him when she saw him, but hoped she could say something encouraging. Something that would prove to him she was willing to take a chance.

"Hopefully, I haven't ruined things between us with my silence. He—"

The door to the store opened and Mona turned. Her breath caught in her throat. Her pulse amped up.

Dexter.

"How?" She glanced at Sumeera before returning her attention to him. "What are you doing here?"

"I couldn't go another day without seeing you."

He sauntered across the room and, like usual when in his presence, heat soared through her body.

"Can we talk?"

Chapter Sixteen

Dexter would be forever grateful for Sumeera texting him earlier to let him know where her mother was. What he wasn't sure of was whether or not Mona wanted anything to do with him, or if showing up had been a good idea. When he had talked to Sumeera twenty minutes ago, she told him he shouldn't let her mother get away without a fight.

By the warm smile on Mona's lovely face, maybe he wouldn't have to work as hard as he originally thought to keep her in his life.

"I have to get going," Sumeera announced. "Nate or Liam will lock up when you're ready to leave. Once you guys go through the place, let me know what you think. If you decide it'll work for the boutique, we can hammer out the details." She started for the door. "Oh, and Dex, I trust you can get my mother home."

Dexter grinned and gave her a nod. "I'll take good care of her."

Once they were alone, Mona spoke. "Dex, I'm sorry for my reaction the other night. You caught me off guard and I needed time to process all that you told me."

Dexter moved closer, wanting so badly to touch her, to kiss her tempting lips.

"I understand, sweetheart. I'm so sorry to put that on you." He cupped her cheek, and caressed her soft skin with the pad of his thumb. She leaned into his touch and hope bloomed inside of him. "I'll never touch alcohol again. I'll never put the people I love through anything like that again. All I ask is that you not let my past ruin what we're building."

"I'm not going to lie, Dexter. I'm scared. I want to give us a chance, but what if something happens to push you to drink again? I don't know if I could handle that."

"Just give me a chance to show you the man I am now."

Mona studied him for a long minute before nodding. "I like the man you are, and I want to see where our relationship goes."

His arm encircled her, and he lowered his mouth to hers. Peace settled over him and renewed optimism filled him. He was right where he wanted to be with the woman he desired more than anyone on this earth. Mona hadn't returned his declaration of love the other night, but he believed in time, she'd love him as much as he loved her.

Hours later, they stood in the checkout line at the grocery store as Dexter paid for a few items. When he had left Mona's place the other day, he thought he had lost her. Thought she wouldn't want anything else to do with him. But as she showed him around the space of her future boutique, she made him feel as if starting the business would be a venture they would do together. Asking his opinion about every aspect of the space, from set-up to lease cost, showed she trusted him, that they might have a future together. She was making him a part of her dream, which meant more to him than she'd ever know.

"Are you going to tell me what you're preparing for dinner?" Mona asked, when they walked through the grocery store's sliding door and out into the chilled air. She slipped her arm through his and snuggled closer as he pushed the shopping cart out to the parking lot. "I could guess what's on the menu with the ingredients you purchased, but when you added the brown sugar to the cart, it threw me off."

Dexter smiled down at her before glancing around the semi-crowded lot. He guided them down their aisle, maneuvering around a car waiting to park in a spot someone was vacating.

"I'll give you a hint. We had this dish on our third date, well at least part of the dish."

"You've counted our dates?"

"You haven't?" he asked in mock disbelief, and she rolled her eyes, smiling.

"I can't remember everything we've eaten."

"I'm hurt. Do you have any idea of the work that goes into planning our dates? Now I find out you don't even remember them."

"Is it chicken stir-fry?" she asked, ignoring his comment. "Oh, I know; brown sugar spiced baked chicken. Right?"

"You might as well give up. You're way off base. As for the brown sugar, it's not a part of the dish. I just ran out."

"Oh, you." Laughing, Mona poked him in the rib. He liked seeing her smile and her playful side. He never wanted to see the sadness he saw on her face the other night. He never wanted to disappoint her.

"I appreciate your willingness to cook."

"I love cooking for you. It gives me a chance to spoil you a little." She awarded him with a smile, and then shivered against him as the wind picked up.

They approached his vehicle. "Let's get you into the truck, and then I'll put the bags in back."

Once the bags were stored, Dexter headed to the cart return a few cars over and left the shopping cart. When he reached the back of his truck, he felt a presence before spotting the dark figure approaching him.

"You think you can just take her from me?" the gruff voice said before stepping from between two parked cars.

What the...

"Russell? What the hell are you doing here?"

"I came for Mona, and you need to stay away from her."

"You let her walk away and now you're trying to control who she sees? I don't think so. I'm here to stay. If you have a problem with that, then go back to wherever you came from so you don't have to watch."

"I'm not going anywhere without her. Mona! Mona!" Russell yelled, approaching the truck. There was an empty parking space between Dexter's vehicle and a small car, giving her ex space to linger.

Dexter stepped in front of him before he made it to the front passenger door.

"You need to back up," he said, not missing the wild look in the man's eyes. Mona mentioned she'd tried getting him some help, for fear something was mentally wrong with him, but Dexter wondered if the guy wasn't high on something.

Before he could stop her, Mona climbed from the truck.

"What in the world? What are you doing here?" She moved around Dexter, but he halted her with a firm hand on her arm. She glanced up at him, and thankfully didn't protest when he held firm to her.

"Let her go," Russell growled. "Now!" He yanked a dark object out of his jacket pocket.

Dexter froze.

Mona gasped.

"Where did you get a gun?" Her voice shook. Dexter tried moving her behind him while he kept his attention on Russell and the small pistol in his hand, but Mona wouldn't budge. "Why are you doing this, Russell?" she asked.

"I told Henry to stay away from you. He's been flirting with you for years, and I'm done trying to reason with him."

Dexter glanced at Mona in confusion. She shook her head. Something was definitely wrong with this guy, and as long as he was waving a gun at them, he wasn't letting her near the man.

"Russell, you have it all wrong. This is not our doorman. This is not Henry. This is my…this is my…my friend."

Dexter's heart sank. Her words cut deep. She meant everything to him, yet she only saw him as a friend.

"He's very important to me," Mona continued. "*Please* put the gun away. I'll do whatever you want. Just put the gun down."

Russell frowned and shook his head. "No. That's…that's not right." He closed his eyes and held the left side of his head as if it hurt. "He's been flirting with you for years," he said, clearly confused and frustrated. His gun hand was unsteady.

"Mona, get in the truck," Dexter whispered.

"But, what about you? I can't—"

"Please, and call 911."

She glanced at her ex, who was still rubbing his head and not paying much attention, but the gun was still aimed at them.

Once Mona was in the truck, Dexter inched closer, almost in reach of the gun. Russell didn't look up until Dexter was in striking distance.

"What are…"

Dexter lunged, ramming his shoulder into Russell's midsection. The momentum slammed the man against a small white vehicle, setting off the ear-piercing car alarm. He grabbed Russell's wrist and they wrestled, grunting, each trying to overpower the other.

"Let it go," Dexter growled between gritted teeth, slamming Russell's arm against the car trying to force him to release the gun.

"Get off of me!" Russell yelled, and they both fell to the ground in a heap.

"Stop it!" Mona's frantic voice penetrated the air.

Dexter glanced back to see her rushing toward them. "Mona! Get ba—"

Pop. Pop.

Dexter winced.

Mona screamed.

Hot, searing pain shot through his shoulder, but he pushed through it, knocking the gun out of Russell's hand before punching him, and banging the man's head against the ground. When Russell stopped moving, Dexter rolled onto his back, his breathing coming in short spurts.

"Mona," he called out, praying she was okay. He tried to sit up, and gritted his teeth. The hot sting in his shoulder hurt like hell. He was pretty sure the bullet only grazed him, but...*damn,* it hurt.

He placed a hand over the wound, trying to even out his breathing.

"Let me go! I have to help him." Dexter heard Mona's voice and relief flooded through him.

She's okay.

"Dex!" She suddenly appeared and leaned over him, tears streaming down her face. "Oh my God. Oh, my God."

"Are...are you okay?" he asked, his heart hammering inside his chest.

"I'm fine. Just don't...don't you move. Help is almost here," she sobbed, but covered her mouth, stifling any other sound.

"Don't...cry." Dexter closed his eyes against the pain, preferring to comfort her, hold her, but his left arm throbbed like crazy. He could feel the stickiness of a small amount of blood on his hand.

Mona planted feathery kisses on his face. "I'm so sorry for all of this. I love you so much. Please...please just be okay."

"I'll be all right. As long as you are..." *Wait.* "What did you say?"

She swiped at her tears. "I said...I love you. I love you so much."

*

Hours later, anxiousness swirled within Mona as she stood in the emergency room where Dexter was sitting on the side of the bed, preparing to leave. With their height difference, this position almost brought them face to face.

"Are you sure you're okay?" she asked, helping him into a button-down shirt that his daughter, Katara, had brought to the hospital. They'd met a couple of weeks ago, when Katara had invited them over for game night with her family. Mona hadn't seen her since then and hated their next meeting had to be in a hospital.

"I will be. How about you?"

"I will be too...eventually." She had been a nervous wreck, even though Dexter hadn't lost consciousness on the ride in the ambulance. Seeing the blood and the pain on his face as they worked on him had her praying harder than she'd prayed in years. She'd been glad to have Katara in the waiting room with her, but Mona had never been happier to see anyone than when Nick and Sumeera showed up at the hospital. For the first time in a long time, she had a family she could lean on.

And there was Dexter.

They hadn't known each other very long, but she was crazy in love with the man and didn't even want to think about losing him.

"You've been fussing over me for the last few hours." With his good arm, Dexter pulled her against him and she rested her head against his good shoulder. He placed a lingering kiss on her forehead. "You're still shivering. Maybe we should have a doctor take a look at you."

"That's not necessary. It's just been a long day."

The cops had arrested Russell before bringing him to the hospital to get checked out. When they questioned her about the incident, discussing the scene out loud reminded her how different the situation could have turned out. Either of them could've died.

All because of Russell.

Mona lifted her head. "I was so scared. I could have lost you. I had no idea Russell would do something like that."

He caressed her cheek. The pad of his thumb was rough against her skin, but she didn't care. The love radiating in his eyes as he stared at her warmed her body.

"I know, but as long as you and I are good, that's all that matters to me."

"I meant what I said earlier. I love you so much, Dexter," she choked out, fighting against the emotion clogging her throat. "If I had lost you…"

"Shh, sweetheart." Dexter pulled her against him. "You didn't lose me. As a matter of fact, I'm not going anywhere. I have to admit, I did have a moment of doubt about us when you referred to me as your friend."

Mona leaned back to look at him. "I didn't know what to call you. Referring to you as my boyfriend seemed a little high-schoolish."

Dexter flashed her a grin that always made her giddy inside. "Then maybe you can call me your fiancé."

Her heart stuttered, and her world teetered. "Wh-what?"

"You heard me. If you agree to marry me, then you can refer to me as your fiancé."

Mona stared at him speechless, trying to determine if he was serious. "You haven't asked me to marry you."

He rose from the bed, wincing, and dropped down on one knee. Her hand went to her mouth, shocked at what he was about to do.

"Mona Lisa Gregory, I know we haven't known each other long, but if tonight reminded me of anything, it's that life is short. I love you, sweetheart. I want to spend the rest of my life with you as your husband. I don't have a ring right now, but I'll get you one. In the meantime, will you agree to marry me?"

Life is short. The words played over in Mona's mind.

For years, she had waited, and dreamed of Russell asking her to marry him. When he hadn't, she'd given up on the idea. Now, this sweet, kind man who she'd only known for a short while, but loved more than anything, was asking her to marry him.

A smile spread slowly across her mouth as happiness bloomed inside her chest. "Yes. Yes, I'll marry you!"

Epilogue

Six Months Later

"That dress is incredible," Johnette said, standing next to Mona in front of the floor-length mirror.

"Thank you. I can't believe this day is finally here."

The last few months had been a whirlwind. Between wedding planning, getting the boutique ready for the grand opening, and attending Russell's trial, Mona had been going nonstop.

Russell's lawyer had entered a diminished capacity plea to the charge of attempted murder, hoping to get the charges against him lowered. After being examined, he had been diagnosed with schizophrenia and bipolar disorder, which his lawyer used as part of Russell's defense. Mona, as well as the psychologist, Russell's driver, and the housekeeper testified on his behalf regarding his mental state and erratic behavior. She was relieved when the attempted murder charge had been dropped to a lesser charge. Now Russell would receive the medical help he needed.

She ran her hands down the sides of her wedding dress. Since nothing about her life had been traditional, she opted for a baby-blue dress that stopped just below her knees. Looking at herself in the mirror, she marveled at the delicate silk garment that appeared strapless from a distance, but wasn't. The sheer material that covered the top of the dress and both sleeves had an intricate lace detail that went down her left arm and part of the way down the left side of her body, adding the perfect amount of elegance. The outfit was one of several pieces that would be featured in the *mature* evening-wear line she planned to carry in her boutique.

She took a deep breath and released it slowly just as the door burst open.

"Mom, you're not ready yet?" Sumeera said, rushing into the room. "You guys were supposed to be at the patio door by now. And where are your shoes?"

"Relax, child," Johnette said, unmoved by Sumeera's frenzied actions. "It's not like the wedding is going to start without the bride."

"Ha! You don't know the Jenkins family. They will start eating before the wedding if we don't get going."

Mona laughed. She could see that happening. The family was known for bonding over food.

Katherine and Steven Jenkins had been gracious enough to let them use their backyard for the wedding; on a Sunday, the day they usually hosted brunch for their large family. When Mona told the matriarch of the family that she didn't want to interrupt their traditional meal, Katherine brushed the comment away. According to her, Sunday brunch was the perfect time for the event. The whole family would be together and could celebrate with her and Dexter.

"You look stunning, Mom, but can you put your shoes on so we can get this party started?" Sumeera grabbed the box of shoes from a nearby chair and pulled one out and handed it to Mona. "Besides, I'm eager to give you your wedding present."

Instead of sitting, Mona accepted the hand her sister offered and held onto her while she stepped into one three-inch heel pump that matched the dress perfectly.

"Honey, unless you plan on giving me another grandbaby, I don't need anything else."

Mona set the other shoe on the floor and stepped into it, but jerked her head up when Johnette gasped.

"What?"

Mona looked down at the shoes. When they appeared fine, she returned her gaze to her sister who had her hand over her mouth staring at Sumeera. Mona then glanced at her daughter, who wore a silly grin.

"What?" she said again, and then it dawned on her what she'd said. "Are you…am I…are we getting another baby?"

Sumeera nodded vigorously, and Mona and Johnette squealed like schoolgirls.

"Shhh! I wanted you two to know before we told anyone else. In six months, you guys will have another baby to spoil."

Mona hugged her daughter and fought back tears. She didn't think she could get any happier, but this news was almost as exciting as marrying the man of her dreams.

*

Dexter released a loud whistle the moment Mona appeared. Everyone within earshot laughed, but all he could do was stare at the beautiful woman who had agreed to be his wife. He didn't think she could get any prettier, but he was wrong. She looked classy and sexy as she glided in step with the wedding march song flowing through the speakers, an endearing smile brightening her gorgeous face.

"Like I said months ago, she's way out of your league," his best man, Sean, whispered next to him.

Dexter laughed. He agreed, but thankfully, she still agreed to be his wife. He couldn't ask for a more perfect day. The fall weather was cooperating, and the women in the Jenkins family, including his daughter, had done a great job decorating the yard. Before getting into place, he'd only had a few moments to take in the décor, including the large white bouquets sitting on white stands at the end of each row of chairs. Now he stood inside the gazebo, staring out in the crowd where at least a hundred people sat, their gazes on his lovely bride.

Dexter went down the one step of the gazebo and captured Mona's hand in order to help her up the step.

"Hi," she said, smiling up at him when they took their place in front of the minister.

"Hi yourself, beautiful."

Her soft laugh washed over him like a gentle breeze, adding to his excitement about this next step in their lives.

"Dear friends and family. We're here to celebrate…" the minister started.

Dexter tried focusing on his words, but all he could think about was how his life had exceeded his expectations. After the accident, he thought he would never be able to find joy again, but he'd been wrong. He had just hit the six-year sober mark; he was surrounded by his family; and most important, he was marrying the woman who was giving him a second chance at love.

Staring at her now, as they exchanged vows, he was glad they had agreed to a short ceremony. He couldn't wait to officially call her his wife and start their new life together.

A short while later, the minister said, "I now pronounce you husband and wife. You may kiss your bride."

"With pleasure."

Happiness soared through Dexter's body when their lips touched. Mona had already made him promise not to get too crazy with the kiss, but he couldn't help pulling her closer and deepening their connection. He hadn't seen her all morning, and he intended to get his fill.

"Save some for the honeymoon," someone called out.

"Yeah, 'cause some of us are ready to eat."

Dexter chuckled against Mona's lips. He knew that voice belonged to Martina. She always had something smart to say, especially when it involved food.

"I guess we should let them eat, huh?" Mona whispered when they pulled apart.

"If we must." Dexter kept his arm around her waist as their family cheered. "I hope you know you've made me the happiest man on the planet."

She touched his cheek, tears lacing her eyelashes. "I love you so much. Thank you for making one of my dreams come true. I never thought…"

Dexter touched his lips to hers again. "I love you too, and I plan on making all of your dreams come true."

The corner of her lips lifted into a smile. "I'm going to hold you to that."

*

*If you enjoyed this book by Sharon C. Cooper,
consider leaving a review on any online book site, review site or social media outlet.*

Join Sharon's Mailing List

To get sneak peeks of upcoming stories and to hear about giveaways that Sharon is sponsoring, go to https://sharoncooper.net/newsletter to join her mailing list.

ABOUT THE AUTHOR

Award-winning and bestselling author, Sharon C. Cooper, is a romance-a-holic - loving anything that involves romance with a happily-ever-after, whether in books, movies, or real life. Sharon writes contemporary romance, as well as romantic suspense and enjoys rainy days, carpet picnics, and peanut butter and jelly sandwiches. She's been nominated for numerous awards and is the recipient of Emma Awards (RSJ) for Author of the Year 2019, Favorite Hero 2019 (INDEBTED), Romantic Suspense of the Year 2015 (TRUTH OR CONSEQUENCES), Interracial Romance of the Year 2015 (ALL YOU'LL EVER NEED), and BRAB (book club) Award - Breakout Author of the Year 2014. When Sharon isn't writing, she's hanging out with her amazing husband, doing volunteer work or reading a good book (a romance of course). To read more about Sharon and her novels, visit www.sharoncooper.net

Connect with Sharon Online:

Website: https://sharoncooper.net

Join Sharon's mailing list: https://bit.ly/31Xsm36

Facebook   fan   page: http://www.facebook.com/AuthorSharonCCooper21?ref=hl

Twitter: https://twitter.com/#!/Sharon_Cooper1

Subscribe   to   her   blog: http://sharonccooper.wordpress.com/

Goodreads:
http://www.goodreads.com/author/show/5823574.
Sharon_C_Cooper

Pinterest:
https://www.pinterest.com/sharonccooper/

Instagram:
https://www.instagram.com/authorsharonccooper/

Other Titles

Reunited Series (Romantic Suspense)
Blue Roses (book 1)
Secret Rendezvous (Prequel to Rendezvous with Danger)
Rendezvous with Danger (book 2)
Truth or Consequences (book 3)
Operation Midnight (book 4)

Stand Alones
Something New
("Edgy" Sweet Romance)
Legal Seduction
(Harlequin Kimani – Contemporary Romance)
Sin City Temptation
(Harlequin Kimani – Contemporary Romance)
A Dose of Passion
(Harlequin Kimani – Contemporary Romance)
Model Attraction
(Harlequin Kimani – Contemporary Romance)
Soul's Desire
(Contemporary Romance)

Made in United States
North Haven, CT
01 December 2021

11827437R00083